CHILDHOOD SWEETHEARTS 2

A Novel

JACOB SPEARS

Good 2 Go Publishing

Written by Jacob Spears
Cover design: Davida Baldwin
Interior Formatting: Mychea, Inc
ISBN: 9781943686605
Copyright ©2016 Good2Go Publishing
Published 2016 by Good2Go Publishing
7311 W. Glass Lane • Laveen, AZ 85339
Printed in the USA

CHILDHOOD SWEETHEARTS 2

1 Smooth and China stood in the same spot at the edge of the lake where months earlier Smooth had thrown the gun that killed two people. Before tossing the gun into the lake, he'd nearly flattened the barrel with a sledgehammer. Even if the gun were retrieved from the lake someday, it would never be fired to conduct a ballistics test.

"Are you ready?" he asked her.

"As ready as I'll ever be," she replied.

They enjoyed the setting of the sun. It would be the last time they would be to seen together for several years. Mr. Hevralesky had arranged a plea deal that would send China to prison for three years.

She knew the severity of her charge, yet she was satisfied with the outcome. She was granted a two-week furlough and was scheduled to turn herself in the following morning.

"I spoke with Donna earlier today," she told Smooth.

"And?"

"The police have no leads or motives. They're saying it was a random act of violence."

Smooth shook his head.

"Are you going to give Roxy the money she needs?"

"That's your call, baby," said China.

"She got it then."

"She really loves you, you know that?"

"Yeah, I know. I love her, too. But not nearly as much as I love your crazy ass."

"You better not love anybody like you love me."

"I don't. Not even myself."

"Does this mean we're back, or that we're going back?" China asked.

"We're back, baby. Back to where we were before the money came."

"That's all I've ever wanted. I'm sure of that now."

Smooth leaned down and kissed her forehead.

"Let's go home, baby," Smooth said.

****

They walked through the front door and Zorro came bounding down the hallway, tail wagging 100 miles per hour. China leaned down to pet him and rubbed his belly. Then she stood and headed for the room.

"I'm gonna take a shower. Want to join me" China asked.

"Hell yeah!"

Smooth watched China undress as he took off his clothes. He could never get over how beautiful she was and how lucky he was to have her. Once in the shower, Smooth grabbed the soap and started rubbing China down without missing a spot. She got down on her knees, grabbed Smooth's dick, and slowly started stroking it. She looked up at Smooth and made eye contact as she slowly took him in her mouth. She looked deep into his eyes as she slowly sucked his dick and played with his balls. It didn't take long before Smooth busted a nut. He came so hard that his knees nearly buckled.

China stood to her feet and stepped out of the shower.

"Come on," she said, grabbing his hand and heading for the bedroom without even drying off.

"This is our last night so I want to make the best of it," she said.

Smooth grabbed China and pushed her onto the bed. Climbing between her legs, he started kissing her, and then moved down and took a nipple into his mouth, moving slowly down her body leaving a trail of kisses. Finally reaching her pussy, he spread her lips open and slid his tongue in. After tongue-fucking her, he started to suck on her clit, as he slid two fingers in and out.

"Yeah, baby!" China said, thrusting her hips.

"I'm cumming, baaaaabyyyy!" she moaned

Smooth moved up after and started kissing her. Looking into her eyes, he slowly slid his dick into her tight pussy. Picking up speed, sliding in and out of her, he stopped suddenly and pulled out.

"Get on your hands and knees!"

China turned over, putting her fat ass up in the air for him. Smooth slid into her hard and fast. Thrusting in and out of her tight pussy, he reached one hand around and played with her clit. She threw her ass back, meeting him stroke for stroke.

"I'm about to cum, baby!" she panted.

Smooth picked up speed, slamming into her harder.

"Ugggghhhh, yes. I'm cumming baby!"

Feeling her pussy tighten took him over the edge, and he shot his load deep into her pussy. Pulling out, he laid down on the bed as she curled up next to him.

"I love you, baby," she said.

"I love you more."

"Damn, I'm gonna miss you so much."

Cuddling up to each other, they talked about their future until they both fell asleep.

2 On the elevator, with hands full of groceries, Smooth wondered what he was going to do. Ever since China went to prison two weeks earlier, all Smooth had done was mope around the house like a sad puppy. He figured he needed to find something to do to keep his mind off of things. Stepping off the elevator and unlocking the door, he stepped inside. China's pit bull, Zorro, jumped up and down, wanting to be petted. Smooth headed to the kitchen to put the food and stuff away with Zorro following close behind. As soon as Smooth set the stuff onto the counter and bent down to pet Zorro, the phone rang.

"Hello," Smooth said, picking up the phone.

"This is a collect call from China, an inmate at Lowell Correctional Institution. To accept the call, press zero."

Smooth pressed the button.

"This call may be monitored and/or recorded. Thanks for using Securus."

"Hey, baby!" China said.

"Hey there. I was just thinking about you."

"Oh yeah? Like what?"

"Like how much I love you and miss you."

"I love and miss you too. It's only been two weeks but it feels like two years."

"I know baby, but it will all be over before you know it," he said.

"Have you seen Roxy or GaGa lately?"

"No, but I'll go check on them tomorrow for you. Maybe all three of us can come and visit you this weekend."

"That'd be nice to see you all. I just wish it wasn't so far away."

"Babe, I don't care if it's 5,000 miles away. I'm gonna come visit."

"You have one minute left," the automated voice said.

"I love you and I'll call again tomorrow."

"Later, love."

After hanging up the phone and putting the food away, he grabbed Zorro's leash.

"Come on, boy!" he called, hooking the leash onto Zorro's collar, and headed out the door.

When the elevator door opened, he saw Miranda talking on her phone. Stepping inside, he smiled at her.

"Okay, I will be waiting for your call. Later," Miranda said into the phone, as she bent down to pet Zorro.

"Hey big guy," she said.

"How you doing, Miranda?"

"I'm good. How about yourself?"

"Need to find a way to keep busy. I thought about buying a few rental properties as we talked about. When would you be available?"

"Anytime tomorrow. Just call."

As the elevator stopped, they hugged, said goodbye, and went their own ways.

****

"Listen up, ladies, its mail call," the officer announced.

"Hamon, Mitchell! Preston, James!"

Hearing her name, China went over to the officer.

"I'm Preston," she said.

"Here ya go," he said, handing her two envelopes.

Looking at them as she walked away, she saw that both were from Roxy and both had pictures inside.

"Alright, ladies, it's time to lockdown for count," the officer yelled.

China headed to her room to read her mail and get ready for count.

"Hey, China, I see you got some mail," her cellmate, Rebecca, said.

"Yeah, my sister wrote and sent some pictures."

"Who's the sexy brother with you?" Rebecca asked.

"That's my man, Smooth."

"He still with you since you're here?"

"Yeah."

"You're a lucky girl."

"I know. Believe me, I know!"

3

After eating breakfast and walking Zorro, Smooth headed out to see Miranda. As he drove over to the real estate office, his phone rang.

"Hello," he answered.

"Hello yourself," Roxy said.

"Oh, hey Roxy. What's up?"

"Well, I finally found a spot for my restaurant. It's perfect!"

"So when are you gonna start getting it ready?"

"I'm getting a list of everything I need together now. Just wanted to know if you wanted to check out the spot yourself."

"Can't right now, but maybe later today."

"Okay, just call me."

"See ya later," he said as he hung up.

Pulling into a parking spot, he got out of his car and went into Miranda's office. As he entered, he saw her talking to the receptionist.

"Oh, hey Smooth, come on back," she said, as she turned and walked towards her office. After following her, Smooth closed the door.

"So how do you want to do this?" she asked.

"Let's do it like last time, where you watch the videos of the properties. That will save time and money."

"Sounds good to me."

"Okay, let me get everything together," she said as she bent over to pick up a DVD to place in the player.

"Damn, girl, you got a nice ass."

"Thanks, but let's keep our minds on the task at hand," she replied.

She remembered how good it felt to have Smooth's hands on her body, but that was the past. He must be horny not having China around. But she put those thoughts out of her head.

"Here we go," she said, after pushing the play button.

Smooth watched as the cameraman walked in and out of each room. About 10 minutes into it, Smooth saw one he liked.

"That one there! I want it."

"Okay, is that it or you want more?" she asked.

"Let's just start with this one."

"Okay, its six apartments . . . $750,000. Still want it?"

"Yeah, I want it. How many apartments are rented already?"

"None, they're just finished painting and fixing it up."

"How much you think I can rent each apartment for?"

"In that area? Probably $2,500 a month. It's a really nice area."

"Well, let's finish the deal," he said.

****

Bored and cruising the streets, Smooth decided to head over to his old neighborhood and see if his old crew was out and about. Turning the corner, he saw Bobby and Banga shooting the shit, holding down the block. Parking down the street, Smooth got out and approached his crew.

"Damn! I'm seeing a ghost!" Bobby said.

"Yeah, me, too!" Banga said.

9

"Both of you funny."

"Nigga, you hit the lotto and forgot all about us," Banga replied.

A car turned the corner and slowed as it approached. Bobby walked over to the car and served the customer. As he came back, he asked Smooth, "What brings you by?"

"Just figured it's been too long and thought I'd drop by and see how you all are doing."

"Hey Smooth," Neko said, coming up the street.

"So how's China doing?" Banga asked.

"She'd doing okay. As you can imagine she's homesick, but she's a tough chick. She can handle it."

"So what you been up to?" Banga asked.

"Not much. Just trying to figure out what I want to do in life."

"Well, you could always come back to work the block with us," Neko said.

"You all still selling nickels and dimes?"

"Yeah, that and a little something else," Banga responded.

"What you mean something else?"

"We moved up to selling some ecstasy and crack," Bobby answered.

"We had to do something. We were losing customers."

"I can't believe this," Smooth said.

"Well, look at you and China. Y'all went on to selling kilos of coke," Banga said.

"Yeah and left us to handle chump changes," Bobby added.

"Listen, I know I did you all wrong, and I'm gonna make it up to y'all. Just give me a few weeks."

"What you gonna do?" Banga asked.

"How would you all feel about moving some major weight?"

"Like what?" Bobby asked.

"Say I can get 30 kilos. What would you all do?"

"I'd say we move 20 in weight and then take the other 10 and cook it up to sell small. We'd made a lot more that way," Banga suggested.

"You know how to cook it up?" Smooth asked.

"Nah, but I got a girlfriend that knows how."

"All right, it's done then. Just give me a week to get the kilos and then you all can do it."

Smooth's phone rang and he answered, "Hello."

"Hey Smooth, I got my list of everything I'm gonna need to open my restaurant, and I'm out shopping now," Roxy said.

"Good. Listen, I wanted to visit China this weekend. Do you and GaGa want to come?" Smooth asked.

"I'm game, but I'll have to ask GaGa, 'cause I'm not sure if she's gonna be working. But I'll let you know."

"Alright. I'll holler at you later then," Smooth said, as he disconnected and headed for his car.

****

"Ten minutes 'til lockdown ladies," the guard yelled.

"Rebecca," China yelled, as she looked around for her roommate.

Spotting her by the television, China yelled for her again. Rebecca looked back after hearing her name. China waved Rebecca over to the card table.

"What's up, China?"

"Grab us a few cups of hot water so we can make some whip and soup."

"Alright," Rebecca said, as she headed to the cell to get the cups.

"Let's count the chips and we will finish tomorrow," another girl said.

"Okay, ladies, let's head to your cells. It's count time."

After returning to her cell, China saw that Rebecca had started making the soup and whip.

"So, how did you do on the poker table?" Rebecca asked.

"I'm up $30."

"Not bad."

"Let's eat. I'm hungry."

After eating, Rebecca told China, "Before you get in bed, we need to talk. I'm not sure how to say this . . . I don't want to ruin our friendship."

"Just spit it out!"

"You promised you will be open-minded and not mad?"

"Just tell me."

"Okay, okay. I guess the best way is just to say it. You know I'm bisexual, right?"

"No, I didn't know," China responded.

"Well, now you know. I'm bisexual and, well, I'm really attracted to you."

"Well, I'm not sure what to say."

"Please don't think I'm crazy."

As if it was the first time she ever looked at her cellmate, she realized how beautiful she was . . . 5' 4", 126 pounds, red hair, and marble green eyes that made her want to drown in them. Breasts the size of softballs, with hips and ass that would drive any many crazy.

Not believing her ears, China asked, "I think you're beautiful, but I'm not sure what you want from me."

"I want to kiss you, eat your pussy, and be your bitch."

"I'm not sure where to start."

"Let me handle that. You just stop me when you feel uncomfortable."

"Okay," China answered.

Rebecca leaned forward and started to kiss China and rub her breast.

"Let's get undressed. It will be a lot easier," Rebecca suggested.

After undressing, Rebecca kissed China.

"Just lay down on the bed."

China had never felt lips so soft and never felt hands so gentle—nothing like Smooth's hands and lips. Rebecca climbed on top of China, kissing her lips and neck, slowly trailing kisses down her body until she reached China's pussy. Damn, she smelled good, but tasted even better. Spreading her pussy open, she worked her tongue in and out while tracing lazy circles over her clit. Finally, she started sucking China's clit while inserting two fingers into China's hungry pussy. China's breath started coming in raspy breaths and gasps. Then her pussy clinched and spasmed as she exploded in orgasm.

"Oh my God! That was so good!" China said after she finally caught her breath.

4 Stepping out of the shower, Smooth dried off and then slid on a fresh pair of Theory jeans, a tight white shirt, and a new pair of Nikes. After dressing, he headed to the kitchen to pet and feed Zorro. Then, figuring he had procrastinated long enough, he pulled out his phone. God, China was going to flip when she found out what he was doing. With that thought in his head, he dialed the number and pushed send.

"Hello?" a voice said.

"Yes, is Jefe there?" Smooth asked.

"One moment please."

"Hello?"

"Hey, Jefe. It's me, Smooth."

"Ah, yes. How are you my friend?"

"I'm as good as can be."

"And how is China?" El Jefe inquired.

"She is hanging in there."

"Glad to hear it."

"Well, Jefe, I called for a reason."

"So what can I do for you?"

"Is our deal still on the table?"

"Yes of course my friend. What do you need?"

"I figure 30 of those things."

"And when would you be by to pick them up?"

"Well, if I left tonight, I'd be there by lunch time tomorrow."

"Okay. I'll be seeing you then."

After hanging up the phone, he couldn't stop thinking about China. God, she was gonna kill him. He was definitely not looking forward to telling her.

****

Smooth called Banga, "Yellow!"

"Hey, I'm gonna come pick you up."

"Where we going?"

"Got to go to New York to pick up that work and you're coming along so you can drive halfway."

"Alright, I'll be ready in 15 minutes."

"See you then," Smooth said, as he disconnected his phone. He then called Miranda.

"Yes?"

"Miranda, I'm going out of town for a few days. Can you watch Zorro for me?"

"Sure, bring him up."

Smooth disconnected and grabbed the leash.

"Come on, boy. Time to go!"

Upon seeing the leash, Zorro's tail excitedly began wagging back and forth, knowing that leash means walk. Attaching the leash, he headed out the door and toward the elevator. Miranda answered on the first knock.

"Come on in," she said as she opened the door.

"Sorry, but I'm in a bit of a rush. I'll catch up with you later."

"Okay, have a nice trip. Me and Zorro will be waiting for you, so bring us both a present."

****

Pulling up in front of Banga's house, Smooth saw him and another nigga he had never seen before outside talking. As soon as Banga saw Smooth pull up, he gave the nigga some dap and headed to the car. After he climbed in, Smooth pulled away and asked, "Who was that?"

"Oh, that's my Uncle Ronny. He just got out of prison yesterday."

"What was he in for?"

"Possession with intent to sell, car theft, grand theft, and a thousand other things. He's a good solid nigga, you'll like him."

"So what's on your mind? I can see the wheels turning," Smooth asked.

"Well, I was thinking we gonna need help. We gonna need people to hustle and grind, but we gonna need muscle too. I was thinking we could bring my Uncle Ronny into the game. He knows all the ropes and could probably teach us something."

"Well, do you think he'd want to help us?"

"Won't know 'til we ask him."

"We will ask him when we come back. But for now, we gotta pick up these keys and have them cooked up."

"Ah man, that' the shit," Smooth said, as he cranked up Rick Ross' *Belly Boy*. Banga leaned back into his seat to nap.

****

"Wake up, nigga!" Smooth said.

"Huh? What? Are we there?"

"Nah, we ain't there, but it's your time to drive. I'm too tired."

"Alright," Banga answered, as he got out of the car and walked around to the driver's side.

"Man, let's find something to eat," Banga suggested, as he pulled out.

"There's a Denny's up ahead."

"That's as good as any place, and it's probably the only place open at this time of night," Banga said, looking at the clock . . . 1:27 a.m.

After they pulled up and headed into Denny's, they noticed two fine-ass redbones coming out.

"Don't even think about it. We on a mission," Smooth told Banga.

"Once they were seated, a beautiful, older white lady came over to take their order.

"What can I get you fellows?" she asked.

"Grand Slam and a Coke," Banga replied.

"Chicken strip sampler and a Coke, no ice," Smooth followed.

"So how far do we have left?" Banga asked, after the waitress was out of earshot.

"About another six hours."

After eating and heading to the car, Smooth said, "Wake me up when we get to New York."

17

Driving while Smooth slept, Banga couldn't stop thinking of all the money he was going to make. He could finally get himself a car and a whole new wardrobe. And he would actually be able to do more for his mother who worked her ass off and did her best.

****

"Why are we stopping?" Smooth asked, as he was waking up.

"'Cause we in New York."

"Where we at?"

"A Flying J Truck Stop. We need gas and something to drink."

"I need to take a piss bad."

They both headed into the truck stop. Smooth went to the bathroom and Banga walked over to the drink island.

"Grab me a Dr. Pepper," Smooth told Banga.

Inside the bathroom, Smooth relieved himself. The bathroom looked and smelled as if it hadn't been cleaned in years. After he washed his hands, he headed back out to the car where Banga was pumping gas.

"Your drink is on the seat."

"Thanks bro."

After grabbing his drink, Smooth slid into the driver's seat. Done with pumping gas, Banga got in the passenger seat. Smooth put on a Lil Wayne C.D. and pulled out of the truck stop, heading back to the highway. Thirty minutes later, began traffic slowing down. Going around a bend in the road, they saw lights everywhere.

"Damn, a checkpoint," Banga said.

"Nah, nigga, it's a wreck. See the two trucks."

Every passing car was rubbernecking to see more. Smooth just wanted to get away from all the cops. Police made him nervous. Even though they were clean, he felt uncomfortable with all of them around.

"Mother fuckers act like they've never seen a wreck before," Smooth said.

"Yeah, I know. Damn, there's a lot of pigs around."

****

Pulling up to the guard shack and gate in front of El Jefe's house, Smooth waited for the guard to come out. Finally, he came to the car—a big-ass nigga with an MP5 machine gun.

"Can I help you," the guard asked.

"Yeah, my name's Smooth. I'm here to see Jefe."

"Is he expecting you?"

"Yes."

"Let me check it out," the guard said, as he returned back inside.

A minute later, the guard returned and opened the gate.

Driving to the house from the fence, Banga said, "Damn, these niggas got major fire power. Like they protecting the President."

"Yeah, Jefe got some beefed up security."

Arriving at the house, two more big-ass dudes with MP5s met them at the door. Smooth grabbed the money out of the back, as he got out.

"Smooth?" one of the guards inquired.

"Come this way," the other guard directed.

Once inside, the guards searched Smooth and Banga for weapons and wires. Smooth figured it was a good practice that he should begin implementing.

Taking them into the library, one guard said, "Wait here. Jefe will be with you shortly."

Banga said, "Damn, this nigga getting that paper."

"Yeah, he is," Smooth replied.

They both sat down to wait for Jefe. Five minutes later, a guard came back and announced, "Jefe's ready to see you all and wants you to join him for lunch. So follow me."

Smooth and Banga stood and followed as the guard led them outside to a table beside the pool where Jefe was waiting. Smooth handed the guard the money.

"Ah, Smooth, there you are. Please, you and your friend have a seat."

Smooth and Banga both pulled out seats and sat down.

"Jefe, this is Banga, my right-hand man; and Banga, this is Jefe."

"Pleasure to meet you," Banga said.

Before anyone could say anything further, two staff members approached with trays filled with sandwiches and chips.

"What can we get you all to drink?" one of the servers asked.

"Just surprise us," Smooth replied.

After a few minutes, they arrived with their drinks.

"What is it?" Smooth asked.

"Captain Morgan Rum and Coke."

"Thanks," Smooth said, as he took a sip.

"Tastes great!"

This was only his second time drinking. The first time was with Miranda. Really liking the Captain and Coke, Smooth decided to start drinking more.

"So my friend, how is China?" Jefe asked.

"She is hanging in there. I'm planning to see her this Sunday."

After bullshitting for another 20 minutes, Jefe asked, "So how many keys you wanting this trip?"

"The usual 30."

Jefe agreed and then yelled for someone named Raul. When the man arrived, Jefe gave him instructions in Spanish. Ten minutes later, Raul returned and spoke to Jefe in Spanish.

"Alright amigos, everything is ready. I will be waiting to hear from you, Smooth."

"I'll call as soon as we get home as always."

Smooth and Banga got up and headed to the car. Smooth said, "I'll drive."

"Alright."

****

They made good time returning to Florida. Once back, Smooth called Jefe to let him know they made it back safely. While he was calling Jefe, Banga called his girl to see if she'd cook up this shit for him.

"So?" Smooth asked.

"She says she'll do it, so let's take her two keys, and start getting this money."

Once they pulled up to the apartment complex, Banga lead the way. Last apartment on the right. Banga knocked on the door. A pretty red-boned chick answered the door.

"Hey Banga, come on in," she said, as she turned and walked back to the kitchen.

"Amanda, this my nigga, Smooth. Smooth, this my girl, Amanda."

Smooth shook her hand and got a good look at her. She was pretty with flawless skin, a little chunky, but in all the right spots.

"So what did you all bring me?" she asked.

"We got two keys of that pure shit," Banga replied.

"How much you gonna charge us?" Smooth asked.

"A grand. Five hundred for each key, and I'll even bag it for ya."

"Deal! When will it be done?" Smooth asked.

"I'll have it ready for ya tomorrow by lunch."

"Alright, we will leave you to it. See you tomorrow," Banga replied, as he and Smooth turned to leave. On the way out, Amanda gave Banga a kiss and then locked the door behind them.

"Where to now?"

"Let's go see where my Uncle Ronny's at," Banga replied, as he climbed into the passenger side of the car.

After reaching Banga's block, they saw Robby with two other niggas on the block. They pulled up and got out.

"What's good, uncle?"

"Nothing, B."

"We need to talk to you for a few minutes," Banga said.

"Alright, let's walk then," Ronny said, after telling the other two that he'd catch up with them later.

"Ronny, we came up on some coke and we gonna start selling big and small. I figured you'd like to come up with us and maybe teach us the ropes."

"What ya all know about selling crack?" Ronny asked.

"Well, I figure it's like selling weed. Bag it up and sell it," Smooth answered.

"You ever sell big? What about small?"

"I've done both, but I sold nicks and dimes of weed, but sold major weight in coke."

"Alright, first off, selling crack is way different than selling weed. Crackheads will sell their mom for a 20-piece."

"Okay," Smooth said.

"So what you think you can just sell crack and get that money?"

"Well, yeah, that's how it works," Smooth says.

Listen, lil' homey. You got to find a few trustworthy soldiers who will hustle the small weight. You gotta find a good spot to sell. You gotta be ready to ride hard or die trying, 'cause each day you will deal with different people. You gotta worry about the jack boys and stick-up kids. Ya gotta worry about the police. You gotta worry about turf wars. You gotta be ready to murk a nigga if they get out of line. Lil' homey, it's a real dog-eat-dog world out there. Just remember, the stress ain't made for everyone, that's why they make sidewalks. If you in the street, you might get hit or ran over. Feel me?" Ronny asked.

"Yeah, I feel ya, but ain't nothing gonna stop me from getting this money."

"And if I gotta murk a few niggas in the process, so be it," Smooth said.

"Alright, what kinda burner you got. Let me see it," Ronny said.

"Smooth looked down and said, "Ain't got one."

"Damn, ya lil' niggas out here with no protection? Ya all crazy!"

"Can you get some for us, uncle?" Banga asked.

"How many ya need?"

"Give us four to start with . . . one for me, one for Smooth, and the other two will be for Bobby and Neko," Banga said.

"Alright, give me a few hours."

****

After getting the burners, they headed to the spot where they all usually sold and hung out. Once they arrived, they met Bobby and Neko who were holding the block down.

"Hey Bobby, you and Neko hop in," Smooth said.

When they both got in, Banga opened the backpack at his feet. Inside was a Smith & Wesson .357, two Glock 9mms, and a Glock .40.

Banga said, "This bad boy's mine," talking about the .357.

"Here, Bobby," he said, handing him one of the 9mm. "And Neko," he said, handing him the other 9mm.

"Last but not least, this beast is yours," he said, handing the Glock .40 to Smooth.

"Listen," Smooth said, "we stepping up the game, so we gotta worry about jack boys and stick-up kids. These guns aren't for show.

They for protection. Never go without it. Take the bitch everywhere, even the toilet. You can't get caught slipping. Y'all understand?"

"Yeah, we got ya," Bobby replied.

"So when we gonna have dat work?" Neko asked.

"We will have it by lunch tomorrow," Smooth replied.

"Until then, stay safe," Smooth told them, as both Bobby and Neko got out of the car.

"Well, nigga, all we gotta do now is find a trap house," Banga said.

"We will look for one tomorrow. For now, I'm ready for bed, so get out, nigga."

"I'll meet you at Amanda's around noon tomorrow," Banga said, as he got out of the car.

Once home, Smooth headed straight to Miranda's to pick up Zorro. Miranda answered after the second knock.

"Zorro was all over Smooth, wanting his attention, so Smooth bent down and petted him.

"How was your trip?"

"It was good. Look, I gotta go out of town again tomorrow to go visit China. I'll be back on Sunday night. Can you keep Zorro 'til then?"

"Sure, no problem. You want something to drink?"

"Sure."

After a few drinks, Smooth was feeling pretty good. Just looking at Miranda was getting his dick hard. Not wanting to do anything he'd regret the following day, he stood up and stated, "I better get going."

"Alright. I'll see you Sunday."

****

Being assigned to inside grounds is basically like having no job at all in prison because out of hundreds assigned to inside grounds, only about 10 work daily. So not having anything else to do, China went to the recreation yard. There were girls walking the track, working out, playing basketball, and playing volleyball. So China set down to watch the volleyball game. China never played, but it looked fun.

"Do you play?" a girl sitting next to her asked.

"No, I've never played before."

"You want to learn?"

"Sure!"

"Well, I got downs, so you can be on my team. We will be playing the winner."

"Are you sure you want me on your team? Like I said, I've never played before."

"Don't worry, it's easy to learn. By the way, my name is Angie."

"Nice to meet you, I'm China."

"Well, let's go. We're up!" Angie said, heading toward the net with China following

China looked at her opponents and said, "Damn, they gonna kick our ass!"

After losing the game, China decided to walk the track. As she passed a group of girls working out, she couldn't help but think,

"Damn, those some big bitches." They got more muscle than most men did. One had arms big as China's waist.

"China, wait up!"

Looking back, she noticed that it was Rebecca yelling for her. China stopped to let Rebecca and another girl catch up to her.

"What's up?" China asked.

"Nothing, just noticed you walking by yourself, so I figured me and my friend would join you. By the way, China, this is Amy. Amy, this is China."

"Nice to meet you, Amy."

"Same here, China."

"Well, let's walk and talk," Rebecca said.

"So what are you in for?" China asked Amy.

"Got busted passing fake checks."

After 20 minutes of talking, they closed down the rec yard. Everyone had to return to their cells for count time and then lunch.

After waking up and showering, Smooth dressed in some fresh Diesel jeans, a tight-fitted black shirt, and brand new Nikes. And the new addition to his attire: a .40 Glock. Heading downstairs in the elevator, his cell phone rang

"Hello," he answered.

"Hey boy, what ya doing?" Roxy asked.

"Going to handle some business, then I'll be coming by to get you and GaGa so we can head up to Ocala."

"Alright, pick us up at the restaurant so you can check it out, okay?"

"I'll be there at 1:00 p.m."

"See ya then," Roxy said, as she disconnected.

Stepping off the elevator, Smooth headed to his Audi A4. Damn, he missed his BMW, but it was too flash and he really didn't need the attention. Plus, the A4 was a really nice car. After starting it up, he headed toward Amanda's to meet with her and Banga. Smooth walked up the steps, headed to the last door on the right, and knocked. A few seconds later, the door was opened by Banga.

"Come on in, B."

Smooth followed him to the kitchen where Amanda was at the stove making lunch.

"Hey Smooth, would you like an egg sandwich?"

"Nah, I'm good. Thanks."

Looking at all the work cooked and bagged up, Smooth said, "Damn, that's a lot of product. Maybe we should have just did one key."

"Well, we got it now, so let's work it, nigga. Bobby and Neko are waiting for us," Banga said.

"Alright let's head out," Smooth said, putting all the work in the big duffle bag.

"See ya later, baby," Banga said, as he grabbed a sandwich and gave Amanda a kiss.

Once at the corner of the block, they saw that Banga's uncle Ronny was talking to Bobby and Neko. It was good that everyone was together.

Grabbing the duffle bag from the car, Smooth and Banga stepped out of the car and joined Bobby, Neko, and Ronny.

"What's up, lil' nigga?" Ronny asked.

"Not much. Got the work here now. We gotta find a spot."

"Alright. Look, I got a duplex out on N.E. Patrician Street. We can use it as a trap house," Ronny said.

"Cool! Let's head over there," Banga replied.

Smooth, Ronny, Banga, Neko, and Bobby all climbed in the A4.

"Damn, nigga, you need a bigger car," Ronny joked.

"Nah, you need to get your own," Smooth joked back.

Two minutes later, Ronny said, "Right there, to the right . . . the white one."

"Who lives here?" Smooth asked.

"I live on the left, and the right is for rent."

"So how we gonna do this?" Smooth asked.

"Keep half the product here. Split the other half in two. Send two niggas to hold down the old block and two to hold down this one," Ronny said.

"Where can we find two more niggas we can trust?" Bobby asked.

"Let me handle that," Neko answered.

"Alright! Well look, I gotta leave in a little, and I'll be out of town 'til Sunday night. Y'all hold it down."

"Tell China we all miss her crazy ass," Banga told Smooth, as he got in his car.

****

Deciding to start moving weight, Smooth called one of his old customers.

"Yeah?" a voice said on the phone.

"I need to speak to Stone!"

He was called Stone because he was always stoned.

"Hang on," the voice answered.

"Yeah, who dis be?"

"It's me . . . Smooth."

"Dot be a miracle. Me waz just tinkin' 'bout ya."

"Well, I wanted to know if you wanted to do business again 'cause I'm back in the game."

"Yeah, me'd like dat. Can I get five birds?" Stoned asked.

"Yeah, I can get you five. Same deal and price as last time. Meet me at the same gas station on Monday at 3:00 p.m. Okay?"

"I's be der!"

"Alright, later."

****

Pulling up to the restaurant, Smooth saw a big sign over the door that read: Roxy's. Roxy met him at the door and greeted him with a hug and a kiss on the cheek. Stepping into the restaurant and looking around, Smooth was impressed.

"Damn, girl, this is nice. I love it!" Smooth said.

"Thanks!"

GaGa came out from the back and shouted, "Hey Smooth!" as she hugged him.

"So when you gonna open, Roxy?"

"All the food and drinks will be delivered Monday and Tuesday, so I plan on opening on Wednesday."

"Well, ya all ready to go?" Smooth asked.

"Yeah, we are ready," GaGa replied.

"So how you been, GaGa?" Smooth asked.

"I've been good. Just working a lot, trying to stay busy. With China locked away and Roxy at her restaurant all the time, I got a lot of free time. So I work overtime to save up and I spend the rest of my free time helping Roxy. What you been up to?"

"Well, I recently bought an apartment building out on N.W. 77th. Trying to go legal, but it's hard, GaGa!"

"Boy, you can do it if you actually put your heart into it. You's a smart boy."

"Thanks GaGa."

****

"Alright ladies, it's 20 minutes 'til lockdown," the guard yelled.

"Damn, I hoped they let us finish this movie 'cause it's good," Rebecca said.

"Yeah, right!" China replied.

Once the commercial was over, both girls went back to watching *Maid in Manhattan*," starring Jennifer Lopez and Ralph Fiennes.

A few minutes later during the next commercial break, Rebecca said, "I'm gonna go get us hot water before lockdown."

"Nah, let me do it. You did it last night," China replied.

After grabbing two of their cups, China headed to the water fountain to get water. There were three other people already there.

"Hey, China, you gonna sign up for the volleyball game tomorrow?" Angie asked China from behind.

"I'll probably have a visit; but if not, yeah, I'll play."

As China got her water, the guard yelled, "Alright ladies, its lockdown! To your cells . . . NOW!"

China finished getting hot water and then returned to her cell.

"Hot! Hot! Hot!" China said, as the cups were full of boiling water.

"Here, let me get them," Rebecca said.

"Thanks."

"So what are we gonna eat tonight?" Rebecca questioned.

"Hmmmm, how 'bout burritos?"

"Sounds good."

China went to her locker where she kept food. She pulled out a bag of Bushy Creek chili, two ramen noodle chili packets, one pack of saltines, two cheese squeezes, and tortilla shells with a bag of Doritos. After cooking the soups and mixing the chili and crackers together, China laid out six shells, put the mix and cheese on them, and then sprinkled them with crushed-up Doritos. Then she folded them and pushed three toward Rebecca. After taking a bite, Rebecca exclaimed, "Damn, girl, these good. Taste like Taco Bell chili cheese burritos."

"They are good, aren't they?"

Finished early and putting the trash together in the corner, Rebecca said, "Take off your clothes. It's time for my dessert."

Watching China undress always got Rebecca horny. When China was finally naked, Rebecca told her to lie down on the bed. Rebecca lay on top and started kissing her. Then she started kissing her neck, moving down to her breasts, kissing and sucking on each nipple until they were hard enough to cut diamonds. She continued to kiss her lower, until she reached China's soaking-wet pussy. Rebecca spread her pussy lips open and started licking all over, and then finally slid her tongue into her pussy. She probed with her tongue, as her thumb slowly circled around on her clit.

"Uhhhh, that feels so good," China moaned.

After tongue-fucking China, Rebecca started sucking on her clit while finger fucking her. China moaned like crazy until she finally reached orgasm, cumming all over Rebecca's hand.

After catching her breath, China told Rebecca, "My turn."

"What do you mean?"

"I want to eat your pussy now," China said.

"I've never had anyone eat my pussy before."

33

"Well, I've never eaten pussy before, but I want to try it."

"Okay," Rebecca agreed, as she took off her clothes and lay on the bed.

Shit, this girl is beautiful, China thought.

China got on top of Rebecca, kissing her all the way down to Rebecca's pussy. Once China reached it, she was surprised to find Rebecca's pussy was shaved bald. Not sure how to start, China licked up and down, and then she spread open her pussy lips and slid in her tongue.

Damn, this pussy tastes good. Sweet and salty at the same time, China thought. After tongue-fucking her, China started to slide two fingers into her. Rebecca gasped loudly. *Shit, I can barely get two fingers in; it's so tight! I bet Smooth would love this pussy.*

As China finger-fucked Rebecca and sucked on her clit, she imagined her, Rebecca, and Smooth in a threesome. Rebecca's started to breathe heavy, her body started to tremble and her pussy started to spasm as she climaxed and came all over China's face.

"Damn, that was good!" China said.

"It wa . . . was . . . amaz . . . amazing!" Rebecca gasped, still trying to catch her breath.

****

On the corner of N.W. 77th Street, Neko and Banga were talking while the new kid, Mark, was dealing with a customer. Banga saw two Puerto Ricans walking up with their hands in their jackets. Automatically, Banga sensed something was wrong with this picture.

34

"Hey Neko! Two Spanish dudes are trying to creep up on us."

Neko looked back and saw them. Both Neko and Banga got ready to pull out their guns. Banga had the big boy .357, while Neko had a Glock 21 chambered with 13 .45 shells. As soon as one of the guys pulled out his gun, Banga drew his gun and shot. The .357 158-grain Winchester Hollow Point tore into the dude killing him instantly. Hearing the shot, Mark turned and drew his gun, at the same time as three bullets ripped into him. The driver of the car burned rubber attempting to get away from the gunplay as fast as he could. Banga's last shot tore half of the Spanish dude's head off. Neko fired into the dead man, emptying his clip.

"Damn, nigga, we gotta get the hell away from here," Banga said.

"Let's split up. We will meet back at the trap in two hours," Neko said.

"Sounds good," Banga replied, as they took off in different directions.

****

Knocking on the door, Banga wished his uncle would hurry up and open the door, so he could get off the street. Finally, Ronny open the door.

"Damn, boy, what's all the banging for?"

"Unc, I just had to murk two niggas."

"What? What happened?" his uncle asked.

"Me, Neko, and Mark were on the corner. While Mark was serving a customer, two Spanish dudes tried to creep on us. Luckily, I was on point. Me and Neko got out okay, but they killed Mark."

"Shit, I told you all about the violence and the turf wars. I just didn't think it'd be so soon. Was there any witnesses?" Ronny asked.

"Nah, nobody seen shit!"

"Are you sure?"

"Well, I didn't see anybody."

"What about the nigga that Mark was serving? He had to see something."

"Shit. I didn't think to look for witnesses."

"It's alright; you just gotta lay low for a week or so and see what happens."

"What do you mean lay low?" Banga asked.

"Why don't you go visit your aunt in Stuart for a week?"

"You really think I should?"

"Yeah, and in the meantime, we need to find more guys and more muscle."

****

"Preston . . . you have a visit. China Preston . . . you have a visit," the guard screamed over the intercom.

"Oh, damn! Oh, damn! Oh, damn!" China exclaimed.

"What's wrong, baby?" Rebecca asked.

"I'm a wreck and my people are here to see me. My hair is a wreck and my nails aren't done, and I'm wearing this crappy blue uniform."

"Just chill out. It's okay. Your family knows ain't no beauty shop up in here," Rebecca laughed.

"Yeah, I'm just tripping. See you when I get back."

China headed outside and walked toward to the visiting park. Once there, China was to be searched.

"Alright, take off all your clothes," the female guard instructed.

After stripping, China was told to open her mouth and run her finger around her gum lines.

"Lean forward and run your fingers through your hair. Good, now turn around. Show me the bottom of your left foot . . . now your right foot. Bend at the waist, spread your ass cheeks, and cough. Okay, you can get dressed now."

After dressing, China went into the visiting area. Right away, she saw Roxy and GaGa, but not Smooth. She ran over to hug her mom and Roxy.

"God, I miss you both so much. Where's Smooth?" China asked.

"He's over there getting us something to eat and drink," GaGa answered.

"So have you dropped the soap yet?" Smooth asked, as he walked up to her with the food in his hand. After laying all the food onto the table, Smooth pulled China into his arms and kissed her.

China's mind was racing: *Damn, does he know about Rebecca? Should I tell him? How will he react?*

All the while, Smooth was battling his own demons: *Does she know I'm back in the game? Should I tell her? How will she take it?*

"So how's the restaurant coming, Roxy?" China asked.

"It's good," she replied. "Should be opening the doors on Wednesday. Just wish you could be there."

At the end of the visit, GaGa said, "Alright you two lovebirds, me and Roxy gonna give you all a few minutes. She and Roxy hugged China, told her they loved her, and left Smooth and China alone.

"Babe, I've got something I gotta tell you," China said.

"Well, same here. I got something I gotta tell you. You go first," Smooth prodded.

"Okay, you know my roommate, Rebecca?"

"Yeah, you've told me about her."

"Well, she's more than a roommate. See, me and her are kind of lovers!"

"What? What do you mean?" Smooth asked with a confusing look.

"She ate my pussy and I ate hers. I'm sorry, baby. Please don't be made at me."

"So what does this mean for us?" Smooth asked.

"I'm still yours, and I want us to stay the same except now we can have some threesomes when I get out."

"Are you serious?"

"Yeah. Listen, I'll be here for three years and we both have physical needs. So if you sleep with someone, I won't be mad. Just don't fall in love with anyone else."

"This is all too much. I gotta think on this and what it means."

"Okay, now what did you have to tell me?"

"I'm back in the game."

"What do you mean?" China inquired.

"I'm back to dealing with El Jefe, but on a bigger scale."

"Are you serious?"

"Yes, I'm dead serious. But now I have Banga, Neko, Bobby, and a few others working with me."

"I can't believe you're back into all that shit after what we've been through."

"Alright ladies, say your goodbyes. Visit's over," a guard announced.

"Baby, I love you and will be back next week," Smooth told China, as he hugged and kissed her.

"I love you, too, boy," China responded.

****

After dropping off Roxy and GaGa, Smooth headed home. Entering the building and then the elevator, Smooth couldn't get China's words out of his head: *Not only is she sleeping with someone else, but also she tells him he can sleep around if he wants. Should I be mad?*

Smooth decided to visit Miranda to pick up Zorro and maybe talk to her. Stepping off the elevator, Smooth headed for Miranda's door and knocked. Miranda answered the door after the second knock, wearing a pair of boy shorts and a wife beater.

"Sorry, I'm in the middle of a workout. Come on in."

If you want, I can come back later," Smooth suggests.

Zorro ran up trying to get attention. Smooth bent down and began to pet Zorro.

"Were you a good boy?" Smooth asked the dog.

"Can I get you a drink?"

"Yeah, Captain and Coke," Smooth replied, figuring it will relax him.

"Come in and get comfortable."

Smooth sat on the couch with Zorro at his feet.

"Here's your drink," Miranda said.

"Thanks," Smooth answered, downing it in three gulps.

Looking at Miranda, he can't help but notice that she was all sweaty and her nipples were showing through the wife beater.

"Damn, boy, you want another one?"

"Yeah, if ya don't mind."

He watched her fat ass jiggle as she walked toward the kitchen. Damn, she was fine. His dick was hard just watching her. *Gotta get a grip on myself*, he thought.

"Here ya go!" she said, handing him another drink.

"So what's got you stressed out?" Miranda asked.

"China."

"What about China?"

"I went to visit her today. She told me that she's been having sex with her roommate. She also gave me permission to sleep with other people."

"So basically an open relationship? A lot of people actually have relationships like that."

"I don't know how to feel about it. And I can't get it out of my head."

Miranda walked up to Smooth, stood right in front of him, looked him in the eyes, and said, "I bet I can get it off your mind."

"Oh yeah! How?"

Without saying a word, she pulled off the wife beater, stepped out of her boy shorts, and got on her knees. She reached out and grabbed his zipper, and then reached in and pulled out his dick from his pants and boxers.

"Looks like he was ready to play!" she said, seeing his dick was at full mast.

After stroking his dick a few times, she put her lips around the head of it and sucked on it while running her tongue over it. She then took the whole thing down her throat.

"Damn, baby, that feels so good," Smooth said, as Miranda began deep throating his whole cock.

"If you don't stop, I'm gonna cum!"

In response, she just picked up speed, sucking harder.

"Ummmm, here I cum, baby!" he shouted, as he exploded in her mouth. It felt as if he shot a whole gallon down her throat.

"We ain't done yet," she said, getting to her feet.

"Lean back" she ordered, as she straddled him. She reached down and grabbed his cock, while guiding it to her wet pussy.

Holy shit, this pussy tight! Smooth thought, as she grabbed the back of the couch and started to ride him. As she went up and down, Smooth caressed her breasts. Her nipples were harder thanks bricks.

She rode him for another few minutes, sliding up and down on his cock, going up all the way and then down.

"Uhhh, Uhhhh . . . I'm gonna cum!" she screamed, while shuddering and shaking.

Smooth started thrusting his hips up to meet hers. As she was cumming, her pussy spasmed and got even tighter. Not being able to hold back any longer, Smooth shot his load deep inside her tight pussy.

"That was so good! I miss this," Miranda exclaimed.

"Yeah, me, too!"

"So will you stay the night?"

"Yeah."

6 The next morning, Smooth woke and smelled something cooking. He got out of bed, dressed, and then followed his nose to the kitchen. Miranda was at the stove in nothing but a bra and panties. Smooth walked over to her, wrapped his arms around her, and kissed her neck.

"Umm, you go sit down. I made you eggs, bacon, and toast."

"Sounds great!"

Sitting down, Smooth pulled out his cell phone and realized his phone had been off since he visited China. *Damn, hope no one important called*, he thought to himself. Turning it on, he saw that he had a shitload of text messages. Scrolling through them, he noticed that most were from Banga. *Better see what he wants*, he thought, as he pushed send.

"Yellow!" Banga answered.

"Damn nigga! Why you been blowing my phone up?"

"Had some problems," Banga replied. "Had to murk a few niggas! So I'm out of town 'til it cools down some. Been worried about you, nigga. It's not like you to go without answering your phone."

"I know. I turned it off when I went to see China and guess I forgot to turn it back on."

"So how is China?"

"She's holding in there. Well, I'll get up with ya later. I got some business to handle," Smooth said, as he disconnected.

"Here is your breakfast. Want some milk or orange juice?"

"Yeah, let me get some orange juice."

After getting his juice, she got her own plate and sat down.

"So what do you have planned for today?" Miranda inquired.

"Got some business to handle and then I'm gonna go shopping."

"What about you?" he asked.

"Just work. Maybe a few laps around the pool."

"I might hit the pool myself later on today."

After finishing eating, Smooth grabbed Zorro's leash.

"Come on, boy, time to go."

Zorro was bouncing around all excited.

"He loves going out, don't he?' she asked.

"He sure does," Smooth replied, while attaching his leash.

"I'll call later," Smooth said, as he headed toward the elevator.

After walking Zorro, Smooth showered. Once he was done, he dressed in a fresh Polo Ralph Lauren outfit with a pair of Bottega Veneta boots. Dressed and ready to meet Stone, Smooth grabbed five kilos, threw them in a bag, grabbed his .40 caliber, and headed out.

****

Smooth was driving his Audi A4 and stopping at the gas station on his way to meet Stone. Zorro was sitting in the passenger seat enjoying the passing cars, while Big Sean's *Play No Games* was pumping through the speakers. Smooth's phone rang, and he answered it without checking to see who was calling.

"Hello?"

"This is a collect call from China, an inmate at Lowell Correctional Institution. To accept the call, press zero."

Smooth pressed zero.

"This call may be monitored and/or recorded. Thanks for using Securus."

"Hey, baby," China said.

"Hey!"

"What ya doing?"

"Fixing to handle some business with Stone."

"Shit, you really are back in the game, huh?" China asked.

"Yeah, running low on paper and no 9-to-5 job gonna pay a nigga like me anything but minimum wage."

"I guess I can understand, but please, baby, please be careful."

"Don't worry, I'll be careful. I got Bobby, Neko, and a few new hustlers doing the small stuff. And I'm doing the big stuff with all our old friends. But anyhow, what you told me yesterday really fucked me up," Smooth continued.

"Well, listen, baby. I got three years to do. And I know in these few years you're gonna have sexual desires and needs. I can't fulfill those needs. So I want you to know that I'll understand if you sleep with someone. I won't hold it against you. Hell, I don't want you to catch a deadly case of the blue balls," China joked.

"So you're really sleeping with another girl?"

"Yes."

"You let her eat your pussy and you ate hers?" Smooth said, getting hard just thinking of China and another girl.

"Yes and I love it. Not as much as I love making love to you, but I still like it. I can't wait to have a threesome with you. Every time me and Rebecca have sex, I think of you and imagine you in a corner watching us."

"I'm hard just thinking about you and another girl," Smooth said.

"So, you're not mad?"

"Nah, I'm not mad, baby. How are your books? Do you need some more money?"

"Yeah, I could use some."

"How much can you spend at a time?"

"We can spend $100 a week."

"Okay, I'll go online to that J-pay thing and send as much as it will allow me to. I know there's a limit, but I'm not sure what it is. Check your balance tomorrow, okay?"

"I will check it and call you tomorrow to let you know if I got it or not. So how's Roxy's doing?"

"She's going nuts trying to make sure everything's done by Wednesday so she can open. The place is amazing. I was surprised."

"You have one minute left," an automated voice announced.

After saying they loved each other, they both disconnected.

****

Passing the gas station, Smooth saw Stone standing beside his car next to the building. Smooth continued passing the station to circle the block and check it out. Not seeing anything amiss, he pulled into the gas station and pulled up alongside Stone.

Lowering the window, Smooth said, "Meet me at the Denny's up the road."

Then he pulled out of the lot and headed to Denny's. Once there, he lowered all the car windows roughly four inches so Zorro would get fresh air. As Smooth stepped out of his car, he saw Stone pull up. Smooth waited for Stone to park, got out, and met him at the door.

"How's it going, Stone?"

"'Tis goin' good, my friend."

They picked a booth toward the back. As soon as they sat down, a pretty blonde came by to ask if they were ready to order.

"I'll take a chicken sampler platter and Coke, no ice," Smooth said.

"I take de Grand Slam and tea," Stone answered.

As the waitress left, Stone turned to Smooth and asked, "So, what dee point in meeting here? Why talk?"

"Well, my friend, I wanted to make you a deal. I give you five keys at $20,000 a piece, right?"

"Yea, dat be right."

"Well, here's the deal. If you buy more, say 10 keys at a time, I will hook you up for $18,000 apiece. Would you be able to handle that?"

"Ya mon, I be able to handle 'tis new deal," Stone said.

"It will continue to be the same product and we will go back to our regular meetings. If you want to raise the amount, call me."

The waitress showed up with their food. After eating and heading out, Zorro was going nuts wanting attention. Smooth hooked on Zorro's leash and let him out. After running around the car to the trunk, Smooth pulled out the book bag and handed it to Stone, who handed Smooth another bag, which Smooth put in the trunk.

"Take care, my friend," Stone said, heading back to his car.

Smooth walked Zorro and then headed back to the car.

"Time to go home, boy!"

7 "You got it, you got it bad. When you're all alone," Usher's song played on Smooth's speakers, as he headed toward the 2200 block of N.E. Patrician Street to meet Ronny and the guys. As he arrived at the duplex, he saw the driveway full on Ronny's side, so he pulled to the empty side. Getting out and heading toward the door, the door opened and Neko stuck his head out.

"What's good, my nigga?" Neko asked.

"I was fixing to ask you the same. Everyone here?'

"Yeah, we've just been waiting on you."

Neko opened the door wide to allow Smooth in. Stepping past Neko and into the room, Smooth saw Ronny, Bobby, and about 10 other dudes. They were all rough looking and varied in age, between 16 and 50.

"'Bout time you showed up," Ronny said.

"Sorry . . . had some business to handle."

"Well guys, this is Smooth, your boss. Smooth, this is the new crew. They have all been hustling for years, and they all know the game. But most important, they not scared to light a bitch up."

"Nice to meet you all. As Ronny said, I'm the boss but Ronny is number two. I look forward to each of us moving up in the food chain. If there are ever any problems or any doubts about anything, do NOT, and I stress DO NOT, hesitate to come to me or Ronny."

"Okay, let's go make this money, boys!"

They each headed out to different street corners.

"Let me holla at you a minute," Ronny told Smooth.

"What's up?"

"All these dudes are the real deal. Keep them happy and they will be loyal for life."

"I sure hope so."

"Well, I'm sure Banga done told you, but he and Neko had a shoot-out with some Spanish people. It's a small-time gang that normally runs over here. This won't be the only time we butt heads. Sooner or later, it's gonna be an all-out war. One of ours already died and Banga is having to lay low. Are you still ready for this?"

"Hell yeah! If they want a war, let's give them one."

"Well, we might get one soon. We killed two of their people. I'm sure they're not happy, so be prepared," Ronny said.

"Don't worry, I will be very careful," Smooth replied.

****

Booker Park off 5th Avenue in Stuart, Florida is the slums. Banga's aunt had lived there for as long as Banga could remember. Banga always liked visiting his aunt and two cousins, Meka and Ham. This visit was going to be like all the others—party time. At the time, Banga and his two cousins were at the park on 5th Avenue watching a basketball game.

"Let's head over to the Cotton Club," Meka suggested.

"Yeah, good idea," Ham said.

"I'm game for whatever," Banga replied.

After arriving at the Cotton Club, they hung out for about 30 minutes when some nigga started trying to get all in Ham's face. Not taking any shit, Ham punched him right in the face. The guy returned a punch, knocking Ham down. Banga automatically stepped in and started beating the shit out of the dude, punch after punch. The next thing Banga knew, two police officers were yelling at him to stop. Not wanting to get tased, he stopped and let them pat him down and handcuff him.

After arriving at the Martin County Sheriff's Office, they made Banga strip naked.

"Open your mouth, run your finger around your gums like this. Lift up your nuts. Turn around. Let me see the bottom of your right foot. Wiggle your toes. Okay, now left foot. Bend at the waist and spread your cheeks . . . now cough. Okay, here, get dressed. Banga put on the bright orange uniform.

If you'll follow me, we'll get you to your new house," the deputy instructed.

The deputy handcuffed Banga. On the way past the laundry, they stopped and the deputy grabbed a bag and handed it to Banga.

"This has two uniforms, two sheets, a bedroll, two towels, and a blanket. Everything you need."

Once they got to A-4, the guard told Banga, "You're in zone 1, room 6."

Going straight to his cell to put his stuff away, he saw a white dude in the cell on the bottom bunk. He was writing. As soon as Banga stepped into the cell, the white dude said, "Welcome to hell, buddy."

"Yeah, thanks!"

"My name's Jacob Spears, but everyone calls me Kentucky."

"My name's Banga."

"I'll step out of the cell and give you some space to make your bed and get moved in."

After Kentucky stepped out of the room, Banga made his bed quickly and then hurried to the phone. Both phones were being used so Banga sat down to wait.

"Are you waiting on the phone?" another dude asked.

"Yes."

"Well, I'm next in line. You can get it after me. I won't be that long. Just gotta see if my people coming for a visit."

"Okay."

"So, what's your name?"

"Banga."

"Well, Banga, my name is Prince Guru, but just call me Guru."

"Will do. Hey, what time do we eat around here?" Banga asked, as his stomach growled, since he missed lunch.

"They feed dinner in about an hour."

"Thanks."

"No problem. Hey, do you place chess?" Guru asked.

"I've played before, but I don't know if I'm good."

"Well, when you get off the phone, wanna play?"

"Yeah, I'll play."

"GURU!" the dude at the phone hollered.

"Gotta go!" Guru said, as he headed to the phone.

Banga sat on the seat watching television until it was his turn to use the phone.

"You're up, Banga. See ya at the table when you're done."

52

"Alright."

Picking up the phone, he dialed Smooth's number.

"Please state your name," the automated voice requested. "Please wait while the call is being connected . . . Please hold while the party you're calling sets up an account."

After a few minutes, the voice continued, "Thank you for using Securus."

"Hello?"

"Bro, you're my dawg. You can always call me. Now, tell me what happened," Smooth asked.

"I was at this place and some nigga started shit with my cousin. So I jumped in; and next thing I know, the damn police are there."

"Okay, so what did they charge you with?"

"They got me with assault."

"You got a bond?"

"Won't know 'til tomorrow when I go before the judge for first appearance."

"Let me know as soon as you get one, alright?"

"Yeah, I'm just glad I left my burner with Uncle Ronny, because I'd really be in shit then."

"You have one minute left," the automated voice stated.

"I love ya, nigga. Call me when you get a bond."

"I will, and I love ya, too, bro. And . . . ," before he said anything further, the phone disconnected.

After he hung up the phone, he looked around for Guru. Banga spotted him sitting with another person at a table in the back, so he headed back to the table.

Once he got there, he asked, "Am I interrupting?"

"Nah, man, have a seat. You're white, I'm black. Banga, this is my main man, Sue Rabbit. Sue, this is Banga."

"What's up, yo?" Sue asked.

"Nothing, what's good?"

"You see it?"

"Yeah."

"So, you new, right?' Sue asked.

"Yeah. Just got here."

"Where you from?"

"I'm from Miami, but I was here visiting my aunt and cousins."

"So where'd you get busted?"

"The Cotton Club."

"Oh yeah? That's my turf. Who's your cousin?"

"Ham."

"Damn, I know him. Just ask him about me."

"I will, is it my go?"

"Yeah."

"So what are you in for?" Banga asked.

"Some bullshit-ass sales charge."

"What about you, Guru?"

"Same thing."

"So what's up with my roommate?"

"He's cool. Spends most of his time writing and working out."

"Time for lockdown, fellows, so head to your cells," a guard announced over the intercom.

"Alright, we will finish this after chow," Guru said.

Getting back to this cell, Banga saw his roommate writing in the same spot.

"What are you writing?" Banga asked, trying to start a conversation.

"I'm writing a book. Well, I'm writing my second book. My first book I sent to a bunch of publishing companies. Right now, I'm just hoping one of the companies likes my book and wants to publish it. My dream has always been to be a published writer."

"So how long does it take you to write a book?"

"Well, it took me six months to write my first one, because I kept going back and changing things."

"So what kind of book you writing?"

"Urban novels," Kentucky replied.

"Urban novels? Are you serious? A white boy writing urban?"

"Yeah, but see, I lived that life. I was out there robbing, stealing, carjacking, and murking niggas. I lived in the fast life, and I killed anyone in my way."

"So what are you in for now?"

"Murder and carjacking."

"How long you been in?"

"I've been in prison for 13 years. But I'm here in County on another charge, because I killed a child molester at Martin Correctional Institution."

"So you caught a body while in prison?"

"Yeah," Kentucky answered.

"Damn, you must have been willing out."

The doors opened and a guard screamed, "Clear count."

"Come on, they gonna serve chow any minutes," Kentucky said.

****

Ronny and two of the new guys were on the corner in the hood that Banga and Neko normally hung out at. But Banga was out of town, and Neko was on a new corner with two other dues.

"Man, I'm telling you that Jay Z owns part of the Brooklyn Nets," one dude said.

"I thought it was the Celtics!"

"Nah, nigga, it's the Nets!"

"Can't you two agree on anything?" Ronny asked.

"Yeah, we both think that Beyoncé is the baddest bitch."

"Yep, we agree on that."

Being almost 9:00 p.m., the streetlights were on and the three were off in the shadows, until a car pulled up and one of them would serve the customer. A car turned the corner and slowed, and one of the two dudes with Ronny headed out to take care of the customer. Ronny watched for trouble. As the dude reached the car, Ronny saw someone pop up from the backseat with a shotgun. Boom! Boom! Boom!

The car then burned rubber and took off. Ronny pulled out his Glock 26 9mm and started unloading into the car. Pop! Pop! Pop! Pop! Pop! Filling the car with holes and busting the back window out, the car finally turned the corner. Ronny ran and checked on his crewmember. But one look and Ronny knew he was dead. Half of his face was missing, and his chest was shredded like hamburger meat.

Damn, this shit getting serious, Ronny thought.

"Come on, Jit. We gotta get ghost," Ronny told the other dude.

****

The phone rang and woke Smooth out of a deep sleep.

"Hello," he answered.

"Hey, boy, you sleeping?"

"Roxy, do you know what time it is?"

"Yeah, it's 7:35 a.m."

"And you woke me at this ungodly hour for what?"

"Boy, don't you know what today is?'

"It's Wednesday, so what?"

"Yep, it's Wednesday, mister. And in case you forgot, I open my restaurant in 45 minutes for the first time."

"Damn, I forgot. Don't worry. I'll be there before ya open."

"Alright, see ya soon."

Smooth hung up and got out of bed. After he finished taking a quick shower, he dressed in a pair of True Religion jeans, a grey Nike shirt, and a fresh pair of Nikes. After dressing, he grabbed Zorro's leash.

"Come on, boy. Let's get your outside."

Zorro came bouncing down the hall. Hooking on the leash, Smooth headed towards the elevator. Once outside, Smooth let Zorro handle his business, and then he brought him back inside.

Once Zorro's bowls were filled of water and food, he headed toward Roxy's.

He made it there at 7:48 a.m. Getting out of his car, he went inside and saw Roxy laying out silverware and napkins on each table.

"Well, look who showed up!" Roxy exclaimed.

"Told you I'd be here."

"I know I'm just so nervous."

"Just cool it. The place looks beautiful."

"Okay, you're my first customer so have a seat. Now what can I get you to drink?"

"Coke, no ice."

"Be right back."

Smooth checked out the menu while Roxy got his drink. She had a pretty good menu, and the breakfast looked good.

"Here's your drink. Are you ready to order?" Roxy asked.

"Yeah, give me scrambled eggs, biscuits, gravy, and bacon."

"Alright," she said, as she headed back to give the order to the cook. As she exited the kitchen, a couple walked in the front door, so she headed to help them.

While waiting for his breakfast, Smooth's phone rang. Noticing it was from Ronny, he answered, "Hello?"

"Glad you're awake. We need to talk."

"Okay, well, I'm at Roxy's new place getting breakfast. Do you know where it's at?" Smooth asked.

"Yea, I know where it's at."

"Good! Meet me here, and I'll buy you some breakfast and we can talk then."

"I'll be there in about 10 minutes."

"See ya there," Smooth replied, before hanging up.

"Here's your food," Roxy said, putting the plate down on the table in front of him.

"Hope you enjoy it," she said.

"I'll be having company soon."

"I will be back to check on you then."

****

Smooth waited for Ronny before he started to eat. After about five minutes, Ronny showed up. Smooth waved him over.

"Hey, Smooth!"

"So what's up?" Smooth asked.

Before Ronny could reply, Roxy walked up.

"What can I get ya?"

"Ummm . . . an omelet, toast, and coffee."

"Alright. I'll be right back with your coffee."

Roxy headed to the kitchen to place the order and grab a cup of coffee.

"You should eat before it gets cold. Don't wait on me."

"Whatever," Smooth responded, and started to eat. "Damn, this gravy is off the chain."

"Okay, here's your coffee. Your food will be out in a minute," Roxy said, after setting down the coffee cup.

"Thanks, Ronny said.

When Roxy left, Ronny said, "Damn, that is one beautiful woman."

"Yeah, she's my girl's older sister; and believe me, China looks better than Roxy."

"You's a lucky man."

"Yeah, I know. So what's up? Why we need to meet?"

"Last night, me and two of the crew got hit. They waited until Buddy was at the car, and then someone in the back seat popped up with a shotgun and hit him."

"He the only one hit?" Smooth asked.

"Yeah, he was the only one of ours. I lit the car up, but I don't know if I hit anybody."

"That's two of ours down."

"Bro, we on the defense, but we need to go on the offense."

"What do you mean?"

"We take the fight to them. Find out where they hang out and then take them out."

"I once read a book that said that 'men are more ready to repay an injury than a benefit, because gratitude is a burden and revenge is a pleasure.'" That's us. We need revenge. We can't just let them keep hitting us one by one."

"So how do we do this?" Smooth inquired.

Before Ronny could respond, Roxy walked up, set his food down, and said, "Here's your food. Hope you enjoy it. Would you like some more coffee?"

"Nah, I'm good. Thanks."

After Roxy left, Ronny leaned forward and said, "When you force the other person to act, you are the one in control. It's always better to make your opponent come to you."

"So where do we start?" Smooth asked.

"We find out where they hang out, and then we hit them hard. After that, we let them come to us if we can."

"How do we find out where they hang?"

"Let me take care of that."

****

"Clear count, ladies," the office said over the intercom.

"Go grab us some seats for the movie. I'm going to get on the phone," China instructed.

"Okay, babe," Rebecca replied.

Once at the phone, she dialed GaGa's number. China stood there waiting for the call to go through. Finally, "This call may be monitored and/or recorded. Thanks for using Securus."

"Hi baby girl," GaGa said.

"Hey mom. How are you doing?"

"Other than missing you, I'm doing well."

"How's Roxy? How's Smooth?"

"Roxy is doing well. Her restaurant opened today. I ate lunch there and, girl, it was good!"

"I bet."

"So what are you doing in there?"

"Not much of anything. I play volleyball here and there."

"Child, I told you to use the time you got to better yourself. Get a G.E.D., take some type of course, get an education while you can, and while you got the time."

"I promise I'll look into the programs."

They spent the next few minutes bullshitting.

"You have one minute left," the voice announced.

"I love you, mom. I miss you and hope to see you again soon."

The call disconnected.

****

Banga looked around while he was sitting in a chair and waiting his turn to see the judge. There were seven other dudes dressed in orange on his side of the room. On the other side were two females in green outfits. One of them was an older white lady. The other was a dime piece, with ivory white skin, long brown hair, and just beautiful. He was busy watching her when he heard this name and snapped back to reality. Standing up, he stepped to the podium. After saying his name and C.F.N., the judge looked at him through the camera while Banga was staring at the judge on the television screen. *Feels weird talking through a camera*, he thought.

"So, you're in here on assault."

"Yes, sir."

"You're not from around here, correct?"

"No, sir. I'm from Miami."

"I shouldn't give you a bond, since you're a flight risk. Do you have family here?"

"Yes, sir. An aunt and two cousins."

"I'm going to give you a $20,000 bond on the condition you agree to stay in Stuart until your court date. Can you do that?"

"Yes, sir."

"Then it's settled."

"Don't make me regret giving you a bond."

"I won't, sir."

Happy at his bond, he sat back down, waiting for everyone else to finish, so that he could be taken back to the zones. He couldn't wait to call Smooth and get out of that joint. Twenty minutes later, everyone was finished. The officers handcuffed them and transported them back to the housing area. As soon as he stepped in the zone, he headed for the phone to call Smooth.

"Please hold while your call is connected."

Ring, ring, ring. Finally, Smooth picked up.

"Hey Banga!"

"Hey Smooth. I just got a bond. It's $20,000, but only on the condition, I got to stay in Stuart 'til my court date."

"Well, are you gonna stay in Stuart?"

"Yeah, I don't want to risk getting locked up again."

"Give me a few hours, and I'll be there to bond ya out. In the meantime, don't drop the soap."

"Very funny, nigga."

"Alright, let me go get ready."

"See ya soon."

After hanging up, he looked around and saw Guru and Sue sitting at a table playing chess.

"So, how'd the bond go?" Guru inquired.

"Got $20,000 bond, so I will be out of here in a few hours."

"That's good."

"When are you two gonna bounce?"

"We'll both be out within a month."

"Look, I'm gonna give you both my numbers. If y'all willing to hustle and need work, I will hook you all up."

"Sounds good," Guru said.

"Yeah, sounds good, 'cause I don't have anything else lined up for when I get out."

"Good. I'll be looking forward to hearing from both of you all."

Banga headed to his cell. Kentucky was in there writing.

"Well, roomie, I got a bond, so I'll be out soon."

"That's good news. I also got some good news. While you were gone, I got a letter. You remember I told you that I sent my book to a bunch of publishing companies?"

"Yeah, I remember."

"Well, one finally wrote back. Here, read this!"

Banga grabbed the letter and read it.

"So this dude, Ray Brown from Good2Go Publishing wants your book? That's awesome. Congratulations!"

"Thanks man."

"Look, I'm gonna give you my number, and I will put money on the phone so you can call. I want to stay in contact with you, okay?"

"Yeah, man. That's cool! The only one I have to call now is my little sister, Heather."

"That's her in all the pictures, right?"

"Yep, that's her."

"She's beautiful."

"I know. I can't get over her being so grown up. To me, she's still my baby sister. Last time I saw her was about 13 years ago."

"So does anyone visit you?"

"Nah, man. All my family is in another state. Out of all my family, only my little brother, Chris, and my mom write me. Well, Heather writes me every blue moon, which sucks 'cause I love to hear from her. But she and my mom live in Muskogee, Oklahoma. So no one is close enough to visit me."

Well, I won't lie to you. I can't visit and I probably won't write, but I will definitely keep money on the phone so you'll be able to call me."

"That'd be nice. Make sure you leave your address so I can mail you a copy of my book."

"Here, let me write it down for you."

Banga grabbed some scrap paper and wrote down his phone number and address.

"This is my cell phone number, so I will always have it."

Grabbing another piece of paper, he wrote down his phone number twice—once for Sue and once for Guru. After writing it down, he ripped the paper in half, went to the day room, and handed his number to both Guru and Sue.

"This my cell phone, so you should be able to reach me any time."

"Bet," Sue said.

"Yeah, bro. I'm definitely gonna hit you up as soon as I get out of here, 'cause I'm definitely gonna need the work and the money."

"You all do realize it's in Miami, right?"

"Good. I need to get out of Stuart anyway. Ain't nothing but trouble and problems here."

"You both can call me any time. I'm gonna keep money on the phone for Kentucky and both of you. But I feel sorry for Kentucky 'cause he ain't ever gonna get out, so I'm gonna stay in contact with him and do what I can for him."

"Yeah, he's a good dude," Sue Rabbit replied.

"Alright, let me go get ready."

"Take it easy."

Going back to his room, Kentucky was still writing.

"Damn, dude, you gonna be a famous big-time writer. Can't believe you got somebody wanting your book. I can't wait to read it."

"I'll get you a copy as soon as it comes out."

"Hey, Kentucky! Do you have someone that sends you money?"

"My mom tries to send me $20 a month, but sometimes she can't. She lives off a disability check so she only gets about $650 a month, so to her $20 is a lot. But other than that, I got no one to send me money."

"Well, on my way out, I'm gonna drop some money in your account, alright?"

"You don't have to do that, man."

"No, I don't have to, but I want to."

Banga heard his name over the intercom.

"Well, that's me. Take it easy and don't forget you can call any time."

"Alright, man, stay out of trouble."

Heading out the door, he hollered a goodbye to Guru and Sue.

Once up front, they gave him back his clothes and personal property. After dressing, they released him. Out in the lobby, Smooth was waiting for him.

"Hey, nigga. Ready to roll?" Smooth asked.

"Nah, I got one last thing to do."

Walking over to the money kiosk, Banga put $300 on Kentucky's books.

"Alright, now I'm ready to go."

After getting in the car, Smooth asked, "Okay, where to now?"

Banga gave him directions to 5th Street and then to Booker Park, where his aunt lived.

"Since I'm gonna be down here 'til my court date, I might as well work, right?"

"Yep, but what kind of work?"

"Figure ya give me one key already cooked up, and then I'll go from there and see where it takes me."

"I'll have somebody bring it up to ya."

"Nah, I'll come pick it up 'cause I gotta go get some stuff from home and talk to my mom, so I'll pick it up then."

"Sounds good to me. Just sucks you gotta stay down here."

"Yeah, I know, but maybe some good will come of it. You never know."

****

"All right, ladies . . . recreation . . . recreation . . . mandatory recreation. Everyone out but the house women. House women, get to work!" the guard announces over the intercom.

"You ready, Rebecca" China asks.

"Yep, I'm ready."

"Make sure the lockers are locked."

After pulling on both locks, Rebecca said, "Yeah, they locked."

"Good, let's go!"

Heading to the recreation yard, China told Rebecca, "Go find us some seats to watch the volleyball game. I'm gonna go get us some sandwiches and drinks. What do you want?"

"An 18 wheeler and a Coke."

"Alright, I'll be back."

China got into the canteen line to wait her turn. As she stood there, she couldn't help but overhear the two ladies in front of her talking about how they were running scams on pen pals. China had heard stories about it, but she didn't have to worry because Smooth kept money on her books. She knew she was super lucky to have Smooth, Roxy, and GaGa. Some people in there had no one. Like Rebecca, she has no friends or family to write and send her money.

"Next!" announced the canteen woman, snapping China out of her thoughts.

Handing the woman her card, China ordered, "I want an 18 wheeler, a big-ass chicken sandwich, two bags of Doritos, two Cokes, a honey bun, and a peanut butter squeeze."

"Anything else?" the woman asked.

"Nope, I'm good!"

"Alright, step to the side and wait for your sandwiches to cook," the woman replied, as she handed the card and receipt back to China. After about five minutes, she said, "18 wheeler and chicken sandwich . . . step up!"

China grabbed all the food and headed to the bleachers by the volleyball courts. She saw that Rebecca had gotten seats at the top. Walking up the steps, she handed Rebecca her 18-wheeler, a bag of chips, and a Coke.

"I got us a honey bun and peanut butter squeeze for dessert."

"Yum, this is so good," Rebecca said, taking a bite of her 18-wheeler.

After they both finished their chips and sandwiches, China opened the honey bun, squeezed the peanut butter on top, split it, and handed half to Rebecca.

"So, you ever thought about kids and a husband?" Rebecca asked.

"Not really. I always had money and power on my mine," China replied.

"I figure it's time for me to find a man and settle down. Maybe have some kids. No more crazy shit!"

"Ya know I never even talked about marriage and kids with Smooth. I don't even know if he'll want kids. We always talked about getting money, a nice car, nice house, and going legal."

"At least you got a man. Hell, I get out in three months, and I have no family, no friends, no place to go, no money, and no job. Hell, I don't even know where I'm going to go."

"Don't worry, Rebecca. I'll have you a place to stay. But you gotta figure out the rest, like what you want in life."

****

Smooth sat at Roxy's restaurant enjoying the house special of chicken Alfredo, mashed potatoes, corn, and a dinner roll. He had to admit that it was one of the best meals he ever had. Roxy definitely knew what she was doing. While trying to finish up his meal, his phone rang. Looking at the display, Smooth saw it was from Ronny, so he answered.

"What's good, Smooth asked.

"We need to talk about a few things. Where you at?"

"I'm at Roxy's place eating dinner. Where you at?"

"At home. Anyway, can ya swing by?"

"Yeah, give me about 20 minutes."

"See ya then."

After hanging up, Smooth waved for his waitress. Seeing him, she headed over and asked, "What can I get for you?"

"Go ahead and give me the check."

After getting the bill, Smooth threw $20 on the table for a tip. Getting into this car, he cranked up Rihanna and Drake's new song *Work* and headed to Ronny's. Once he arrived, Smooth went to the door. As he was about to knock, the door of the duplex next door opened, and Ronny stuck his head out.

"Over here, lil' nigga."

"When did you move over here?" Smooth asked, as he hopped the little divider.

"I moved over here today. Come on in."

"The whole operation move or just you?"

"Just me. I got tired of constantly getting woken up at all hours, plus I figured it's best to have my own place that don't have any heat in it, in case it got raided."

"I can understand that. So what did we need to talk about?"

"A few things, but first would you like something to drink?"

"I'll take a rum and Coke, if you have it."

"Got some Bacardi, but no Coke. What about Mountain Dew?"

"I'll try it."

"Have a seat."

After handing Smooth his drink, Ronny sat in a recliner. Smooth took a sip of his drink.

"Damn, this is good," Smooth said, taking another sip.

"First order of business . . ." Ronny got up, grabbed a bag from a closet, and handed it to Smooth. "This belongs to you. Everybody already got their cut. It's $42,000. Next order of business is that we need more product A.S.A.P.!"

"Alright, you all doing good. I'll have you more product tomorrow. Can you hold out 'til then?"

"Yeah, we can stretch 'til then. These crackheads going crazy over this product. Must be some good shit!"

"Have you found out anything on these damn Mexicans or whatever they are?"

"Nothing yet, but I got people working on it. I will let you know as soon as I find out. Now next order of business. I got a big-time club owner who wants to buy two keys. He's having a grand opening of a new club tomorrow called Club Rage. He wants us to come."

"Ronny, you forget I'm only 17. I can't get in a club."

"Leave that me. I'll get you in. You just be here ready to go at 8:00 p.m. tomorrow."

"Alright, I'm gonna go take care of some business. I'll catch up with you tomorrow."

"Be safe."

8 After leaving Ronny's, Smooth swung by his place to walk Zorro and let him do his thing. He then grabbed two keys and headed to Amanda's place, hoping she was there. When he got to her apartment complex, he let himself in and went to the last door on the right. He knocked twice, but there was no answer. He thought she wasn't home. But he decided to give it one more knock. As he reached out to knock one more time, the door opened. Amanda was standing there with only a towel wrapped around her.

"Hey Smooth. Sorry, I was in the shower."

"Nah, I'm sorry. I didn't know you was busy. I would have called first, but I didn't have your phone number."

"It's alright. Come on in. Where is Banga?"

"He's out of town for a while. I hope you don't mind me coming by, but I need to get a few more of those things cooked up."

"No problem. Let me go get dressed. I will be right back."

Five minutes later, she came back out wearing a pink spaghetti-strap shirt that showed off a lot of cleavage and a pair of tight, short-shorts with "Juicy" written on the ass. Smooth was surprised at how beautiful she looked. Well, not beautiful but SEXY and definitely juicy!

"Let's go into the kitchen and get started."

Once in the kitchen, she reached into a cabinet and pulled out a few boxes of baking soda.

"Luckily, I always keep a supply of this stuff."

"So, how'd you learn to do this?" Smooth inquired.

"I had a boyfriend who was a small-time dope dealer. He taught me how to cook it up, weigh it, and bag it up."

"What happened to him?"

"He was killed in a drive-by shooting."

"Sorry to hear that."

"Why, it's not your fault."

"Well, I guess I'm gonna leave so you can do your thing."

"I can cook and talk at the same time, so why don't you keep me company? Unless you got something better to do."

"Nah, I ain't got nothing to do."

"Good. Now before I start, can I get you something to drink?"

"A rum and Coke, if you got it."

"Nah, but I got some Smirnoff Ice mixed drinks."

"Alright."

After she handed him a bottle, he opened it, took a drink, and said, "Not bad!" He was becoming a real drinker.

"So, how long have you been with Banga?"

"I'm not with him. We are just good friends; and sometimes we have no ties, just sex times. But we are not together and we haven't had sex in months. He's with some girl over in Hollywood last time I knew."

"So what about you? Got a man?"

"Nope, no man! All I do is work, come home, and watch TV. I lead a boring life."

"So, where do you work?"

"I'm a nurse."

"Oh yeah?"

"Yep, been working at the hospital for six years."

"How old are you?" he asked, thinking she looked no older than 21.

"I'm 32. Why, how old do I look?"

"No older than 21."

"Well, I'll take that as a compliment. Thanks."

As she was standing at the stove with her back to him, he oouldn't help but stare at her ass, It was nice. Just looking at it was making him hard. He daydreamed about going over there and pulling her shorts down, bending her over the stove, and fucking her doggy style. His dick was so hard he was afraid it was gonna bust out of his pants.

"Need another drink?" she asked, as she turned around.

"Yes, please."

She went to the refrigerator, grabbed another bottle, and handed it to him. As she handed him the bottle, she looked him up and down and couldn't help but see his massive hard-on. She reached down to touch it and asked, "Did I do that?"

"Yes, you did."

"Want me to fix it?"

"How?"

Without another word, she got on her knees, put his gun on the table, and then unzipped and unbuckled his pants. She reached in his boxers and pulled out his fully erect penis.

Damn, this is huge! she thought out loud.

She wrapped her hand around his cock and started to slowly stroke it, while she licked the pre-cum off. Then she put her lips around his huge cock and stated to suck, while taking more and more of him into her mouth. Swallowing so she could deep-throat him, she finally got his whole cock into her mouth. Smooth grabbed her head and started to fuck her mouth like a pussy. Her head game was so good that he couldn't help but to bust a nut, shooting his load down her throat. After swallowing all his cum, she stood up and pulled off her shirt and shorts. Smooth turned her around and bent her over the counter. He got on his knees and ate her pussy from the back, while sliding a finger into her ass. After she came, and her knees started to buckle, Smooth stood up and slid his cock into her waiting pussy. Her pussy was so tight that he knew he wouldn't be able to last long, so he reached around and massaged her clit while fucking her doggy style. It was hard to keep pace, but he soon had her cumming again. He picked up the pace and fucked her harder and faster, sliding his big dick in and out of her tight pussy until he exploded deep inside her.

Afterwards, they took a shower and then finished cooking up and bagging the product. As he was getting ready to leave, she convinced him to stay the night.

****

The next morning, Smooth woke up to Amanda sucking his dick, and she was doing a hell of a job. Before he came, she stopped and climbed on top, straddling him cowgirl style. She started to ride him up and down. Smooth leaned forward and took a nipple into his mouth, while using his right hand to play with her other one. She started to breath hard.

"Aggh, I'm fixing to cum," she said, as she picked up speed.

Her whole body stated to vibrate, as her pussy spasmed and her eyes clouded over in pure bliss. Smooth grabbed her and rolled them both over so he was on top. He grabbed her feet and put them on his shoulders, leaned forward, and started to slide his dick in and out. Pulling his dick out until only the head was in, he then slid all the way back in. Finally, not being able to hold back, he came inside her and then rolled off to catch his breath.

She set up on one elbow and said, "Take a shower and get dressed while I start breakfast."

"Sounds good."

Once out of the shower and dressed, he grabbed his cell phone and was surprised to see that it was already 11:30 a.m. While in the kitchen eating his packages and sausage, Amanda asked for his phone. He handed it to her curious to see why she wanted it.

"There . . . now you have my phone number," she said, handing it back to him.

"I'm sorry to eat and run, but I got to go," Smooth announced.

"It's all good!"

After giving her a kiss, he headed out and went to Ronny's. Once there, he grabbed the duffle bag out of the back seat and walked up to the door. It opened after the first knock.

"Come on in," Ronny said, stepping to the side to let him by.

Handing the bag to Ronny, Smooth said, "Here's the product."

"Bro, look . . . I got something for you," Ronny said, while picking up an envelope and handing it to Smooth.

Inside were two copies of a driver's license. He pulled them out and noticed that both of them had pictures that looked just like hm.

"Pick one to use tonight. And I'll keep the other one in my safe for emergencies."

"Sounds good," Smooth responded, picking one and handing the other back to Ronny.

"Don't forget, Smooth, 8:00 p.m. tonight and bring the two keys."

"I'll be there."

"As he walked back to his car, his cell phone rang. Looking down, he saw it was Miranda.

"What's up?" he answered.

"Just thought you'd like to know we closed and finished on the apartments, so you are now officially the owner of six apartments."

"That's great! Thanks."

"Have you decided what you're gonna do with them?"

"What do you mean?"

"Well, you can sell each apartment or you can rent them out."

"I want to keep two and rent the other four."

"Are you gonna take an ad out in the paper, or would you like my company to take care of it?"

"I'd like you to take care of it."

"Okay, stop by and I'll give you a master key to all six apartments. You can then pick which two you want to keep for yourself."

"I'm on my way."

****

After getting the master key from Miranda, Smooth checked out the apartments and decided to keep units five and six on the top floor. Deciding he wanted better locks on the doors, he pulled out his smart phone and looked up locksmiths. After finding one, he headed downstairs to wait for the locksmith, who showed up about 20 minutes later.

"You the one who needed a locksmith?"

"Yeah."

"Well, point me in the right direction."

"Follow me," Smooth said, leading the way.

After they reached the apartments, the locksmith asked him what kind of locks he wanted.

"The best," Smooth replied.

"Well, we got the Goji system, which has an LED display that flashes a personal greeting as you approach the door. It also has a built-in camera that takes pictures of everyone who approaches the door and sends it straight to your smart phone."

"That's what I want on apartments five and six. How long will it take to install?"

"Give me an hour," the locksmith answered.

Smooth sat in his car watching a movie on his iPhone 6 while the locksmith worked. After he finished, and Smooth paid him, Smooth tried out the locks and then headed to Roxy's for dinner.

****

Once at Roxy's, he went inside and noticed the place was packed.

Heading in, a waitress stopped him and said, "Sorry, sir, but we're full."

"Is Roxy here?"

"Yes, but as you can imagine, she's busy."

Before he could respond, he saw Roxy heading toward them. Once there, she asked, "Carla, what's the problem?"

"I was explaining to this man that we're full."

"Carla, this is Smooth, the one I told you to reserve a table for."

"Oh, I'm sorry. Follow me, sir."

"I'll be with you in a minute, Smooth," Roxy said, going over to another table.

Once seated, Carla handed him a menu and asked what he wanted to drink.

"A Coke, no ice."

"I'll be right back."

Looking at the menu, he decided on chicken parmesan.

"Here's your drink. Are you ready to order?"

"Yeah, chicken parmesan, please."

After the waitress left, Roxy came over and sat down.

"Looks like business is doing well. How'd you know to reserve a table for me?"

"I didn't. This is your table. It will always be reserved for you, so it will always be open for you."

"Thanks, Roxy. So you want to visit China with me this week?"

"Can't! I'll be working, but maybe next week."

"Okay."

"Well, let me get back to work. Hope you enjoy your food. If you need anything, let me know."

Once he finished his meal, he laid $20 on the table and went outside to his car. After climbing in, he turned on the radio. Fetty Wap's *679* came over the speakers. On his way home, he stopped by the gas station to fill up. He then went home to get ready for the night. As soon as he walked in, Zorro came running. Jumping on to Smooth, he almost knocked him over. *Damn, this dog's getting big*, Smooth thought. Grabbing the leash, Zorro went nuts, bouncing all over the place.

"Sit still a minute, so I can hook this thing on. There! Now let's go!"

Getting on the elevator, they went downstairs and outside. Once outside, Zorro took off leading the way. After 10 minutes, Smooth looked at his watch.

"Alright, time to go back in."

Back into the apartment, he hopped in and took a quick shower. Then he dressed in a black Burberry suit with black snakeskin boots. Dressed and ready to go, Smooth grabbed a bag and put two keys in it. He then was out the door to go pick up Ronny. As soon as he pulled into Ronny's driveway, Ronny came out dressed in a Bottega Veneta three-piece suit.

Looking at his Fossil touch-screen smart watch, Smooth asked, "Straight to the club?"

"Yeah, they will be looking for us."

"You're dressed nice there, pimp!"

"You, too!" Ronny acknowledged.

Pulling up to the club, they saw the line was already bending around the corner.

"Damn, that line's long!" Smooth said.

"Yep! Good thing we don't have to wait. You got the two keys?"

"In the trunk."

"Grab it and let's go."

After getting the bag out, they headed toward the door, ignoring the line.

Once they got to the door, a big-ass nigga ordered, "Get in line."

"My name's Ronny. Mac is expecting us."

"Oh, sure. Go right on into the V.I.P. section, and I'll let him know you're here," he responded, pulling out a walkie-talkie.

The place was jam-packed inside. Fine-ass women were everywhere. Once in the V.I.P. section, a server asked, "What would you like to drink?"

"Bring us a bottle of Fireball," Ronny ordered.

"I'll take a bottle of Captain Morgan."

"Be right back, gentlemen," she said, as she walked away.

Several minutes later, the server returned with their bottles. As she was leaving, a white dude in a nice suit came in and said, "Mac's waiting, so please follow me, gentlemen."

They followed him up some stairs and to the second door on the left. The white dude knocked twice, opened the door, and then stepped away, allowing Smooth and Ronny to enter the room. Once inside, another white dude behind a desk stood up.

"Glad you could make it, Ronny."

"Hey Mac! This is Smooth. Smooth, this is Mac."

"You got the product?"

"Yep, right here," Ronny replied, retrieving the bag from Smooth and handing it to Mac.

"Good, now have a seat. Joe, get the money," Mac said to the guy at the door.

They made small talk for the next five minutes until Joe returned with the money. They stood up to leave.

"Hope you all enjoy your night. I'll be in touch."

They headed back to the V.I.P. section.

"Let me go put this in the car. I'll be right back," Smooth said.

After putting up the money and coming back inside, Smooth saw a fine-ass redbone chick at the bar all by herself. He walked up to her and asked, "Would you like to dance?"

"Sure," she answered.

As she stood up, Smooth thought she had curves for days. After dancing two songs, he led her to the V.I.P. section where Ronny had some chick grinding on him.

Sitting down on the leather couch sideways, so he could face Red, he said, "My name's Smooth."

"I'm Jasmine."

"Here, want a drink?" he asked her, handing her the bottle of Captain Morgan he left on the table.

"Sure," she answered, taking a drink straight from the bottle. She handed it back to him.

They both talked and drank. Smooth was really feeling the booze.

****

Stirring from a deep sleep, Smooth tried to open his eyes, but they felt like they weighed 100 pounds. He felt a cool breeze on his skin, as he heard sirens getting closer. Finally, he opened his eyes and looked around. The digital clock read 3:44 a.m.

"Where the hell am I?" he asked himself.

"Uhhhhhh," sounded someone next to him, throwing an arm around him.

Now it was coming back to him. He met a chick at the club, drank too much, and went home with her. Getting out of bed as quietly as possible, he started to dress.

"Leaving so soon?" a sleepy voice asked.

"Yeah. Sorry, but I got to get home."

"It's all good. Let yourself out. I'm going back to bed."

After getting back to his place, he lay down and went right to sleep until the phone woke him up. Looking at the display, he saw it was Ronny . . . and it was 1:00 p.m.

"Yeah!" Smooth answered.

"Hey Smooth. Just wanted to make sure you made it home."

"Yeah, I made it home. I'll holla at ya later. I got to get up and handle some business."

"Alright, hit me up later."

9 Standing at the counter making a sandwich and thinking about China, Smooth's thoughts were interrupted when his phone rang. Looking at the screen, he saw it was Banga.

"Waz up, nigga?" he answered.

"Not much, just cooling. What's good?"

"Can't call it."

"Look, I'm out of product. I need to re-up."

"Well, I'm going to visit China tomorrow. I'll swing by and drop some off. How much you need?"

"Give me like two or three of them things. I got your money for the other two."

"Expect me about 3:00 p.m. alright?"

"Yeah, sounds good. Later."

After Smooth hung up, he went into the bedroom to get dressed. He put on black True Religion jeans, an Affliction shirt, and Nikes. He decided to check up on Miranda, so he headed to her office to surprise her with some flowers. Arriving at her office, he grabbed the flowers he got on his way over.

Once inside, he asked the receptionist, "Is she in?"

"Yeah. I'll buzz her."

"No, let me surprise her."

"Okay."

Walking to her door, he slowly opened it and stepped inside.

Startled, she looked up. Seeing Smooth with flowers made her break into a big smile.

"Come on in, handsome!"

He stepped in, closing the door behind him.

"How you doing?"

"Good, now that you stopped by."

"I thought I'd drop in and surprise you."

"Well, I'm glad you did."

"So, are you busy or can you take a lunch break?"

"Where we going?"

"I figure the Olive Garden. Haven't eaten there in a while."

"Okay, let's go!"

In the waiting area, Miranda tells the receptionist that she's taking an early lunch.

"Let's take my car," Smooth suggests, heading for this Audi A4.

After opening the passenger side door for Miranda, Smooth ran around to the driver's side and climbed in.

"You can pick out a CD to listen to."

"Oh, shit. You got a lot of CDs."

"Yeah, every time I turn around, I'm buying another new CD."

A few minutes later, Usher's voice comes through the speakers, "You got it! You got it bad, when you're all alone . . ."

"I love this song," Miranda said.

"Me, too."

Arriving at the Olive Garden, Smooth headed around to the passenger side to open Miranda's door, but she had already opened it and stepped out of the car. So he headed to the front of the restaurant to open that door instead. He was trying to be the perfect gentleman. Once inside, the hostess showed them to their table.

"What can I get you two to drink?"

"Coke, no ice," Smooth said.

"I'll take a Diet Coke, please."

"Be right back with your drinks," the server replied.

They both picked up their menus and started to figure out what to get. The waitress came back with their drinks.

"Are you ready to order?"

"Sure. I'll take a small pepperoni pizza with bread sticks," Miranda said.

"Guess I'll have the same."

After the waitress left, they started to chat.

"Well, I went by the apartments. I want numbers five and six for myself. I already had new locks put on them. Not sure what I'm gonna use them for, but I'll think of something."

"I'll put the other four up for rent," Miranda suggested.

"Oh, before I forget, I'm going out of town for a few days. Can you watch Zorro again?"

"Sure can. I enjoy his company. Might have to get a dog of my own soon."

"Zorro is a good dog. And he's getting so big!"

"I know. He is growing fast," Miranda agreed.

The waitress returned, interrupting their conversation.

"Here's your food," she said, as she set down the pizza. Miranda started eating as soon as the food hit the table.

"I missed breakfast this morning."

"I can tell," Smooth joked.

"Shut up and eat!"

After they both finished their meals, Smooth got the check. On the way out, Smooth held open the door for Miranda, as well as the passenger door of his car.

"Thanks," she said.

Once back in the car, Miranda announced, "I'm still hungry."

"Why didn't you get more food?"

"'Cause that's not what I want to eat."

"Well then, what do you want to eat?"

"This!" she said, reaching over and grabbing his dick.

Even though the windows were dark tinted, Miranda still looked around. She then turned in her seat so she could undo Smooth's pants. Reaching in his pants, she pulled out his still soft dick. She leaned over and took his penis into her mouth, sucking on the head of his dick while rolling her tongue over it. Slowly but surely, his dick got hard. Once it was fully erect, she began sucking his cock while slowly massaging his balls. Miranda was making sexy moans while she was sucking his cock. She was really deep throating him.

"Baby, that feels so good. I'm gonna cum if you don't stop soon."

"Mmmmm . . ." she moaned, picking up speed.

Not being able to hold back any longer, Smooth started to cum in her mouth. She kept going, swallowing everything. Once done, she sat up.

"I'm full now!" she said, laughing.

"My turn," he replied.

"Oh, I gotta get back to work. You can repay the favor tonight."

"I'm gonna be out of town, remember?"

"I'll still be here when you get back."

Starting up the car and putting it into gear, he headed back to drop off Miranda. He then went back to his apartment to pack and get ready.

****

After showering and dressing, Smooth grabbed two keys and put them in a bag for Banga. He figured since he was going out of town, he'd drop by, see Banga, and drop off some product. Since he was going to Ocala to see China, he figured that might as well head to New York while he was out of town. So he picked up his phone and dialed.

"Hello?"

"Yes, this is Smooth. I need to talk to Jefe."

"One minute, please."

"Hello?"

"Hey, Jefe. It's Smooth."

"Hello, my friend. How are you?"

"I'm good. Look, I'm gonna need another 30."

"Okay, when will you be here?"

"Sunday, about lunch time."

"See you then, my friend."

Disconnecting the call, he decided to hit up Ronny.

"Yeah?"

"Ronny, what's good?"

"Nothing. Just making that money."

"Well, look, I'm going out of town to visit China and the re-up. Are you all gonna be straight?"

"Yeah, we'll be good."

Smooth sat down on the couch for a few minutes. The next thing he knew, he was being awakened up by someone knocking on his front door. Getting up, he went over to answer the door. When he opened it, he saw Miranda standing there.

"Figured I'd stop by and grab Zorro to save you a trip upstairs."

"Thanks," Smooth said, as he headed to the kitchen where Zorro was lying beside his water bowl. Grabbing the leash, Zorro jumped up with excitement. "Here!" Smooth said, handing the leash to Miranda.

After connecting the leash, she headed for the door.

"See you when you get back."

"Alright."

After Miranda left, Smooth grabbed his bag and headed downstairs to his car. Once inside, he pulled out his phone and dialed Banga.

"Yellow?"

"I'm on my way."

"Good. Call me when you get here, and I'll give you directions."

"You got it."

****

Upon entering Stuart, Florida, Smooth dialed Banga.

"Yellow?"

"I'm in Stuart on 5th Street."

"Good. Keep going until you get to a place on the right called, The Pool Room. I'll be outside waiting for you."

"Okay," Smooth responded, as he hung up.

A few minutes later, he almost missed it, but he spotted Banga leaning against a wall with two others. Pulling into the parking lot, Smooth noticed that the two people with Banga were a cute girl and a short, skinny guy. They each walked over and got in Smooth's car. Banga was up front in the passenger side, the girl was in the back behind Banga, and the guy sat behind Smooth.

"What's up, nigga?" Banga said.

"How you doing? Got a court date yet?"

"I'm good, but no court date. Smooth, these are my cousins, Ham and Meka. Ham . . . Meka . . . this is my dawg, Smooth."

"Nice to meet you all," Smooth replied.

"Did you bring that work?" Banga asked.

"Yeah, it's in the trunk. You got that money?"

"Yep. Let's go get it. Pull out of here and go right."

A few minutes later, they pulled up to an apartment complex.

"Come on in," Banga said.

Smooth grabbed the bag with the two keys and followed them inside. Once inside, Banga reached behind a couch and pulled out a book bag.

"Here is your money," Banga said, handing him the bag. Smooth handed him the bag in return with the two keys.

"You in a rush or you got time to hang out?"

"Nah ain't no rush. Why, what's up?"

"Let's all go to the Cotton Club."

****

At the Cotton Club, drinks in hand, Banga and Ham were chatting up two hotties. He and Meka were talking at the bar.

"So where you from?" Meka asked.

"Born and raised in Miami."

"You like it there?"

"Yeah. Ain't ever gonna leave. What about you?"

"Born and raised right now in Stuart. But unlike you, I want to get away from here. I hate Stuart."

"Where would you like to go?"

"I don't know. Probably somewhere up north out of Florida. Maybe Atlanta."

"I've passed through Atlanta, but I'm not sure I'd want to live there."

"You've passed through? Do you travel a lot?"

"Nah, not a lot, but I go up to New York every month or two."

"Every month or two? That's a lot," she laughed.

She had a real sexy laugh. She was cute, but not his type. She was too dark and her hair was too short. But after a few drinks, she was looking better and better.

"Well, it's time for me to leave. Need a ride somewhere?"

"Nope, but I'd like to ride you," she laughed.

"Maybe next time, boo!"

After saying bye to Banga and Ham, Smooth got in his car and took off. Next stop . . . Ocala.

Damn, I drank too much, Smooth thought out loud.

Reaching Ocala, Smooth pulled into the first hotel he saw—a Holiday Inn. Going inside, he didn't see anybody, so he rang the bell. A moment later, an older Spanish woman came out from the back.

"How can I help you?"

"I need a room for the night."

"Just you?"

"Yeah, just me."

"Okay, that'll be $68."

After paying her, she handed him a key card.

"Room 112. Enjoy your stay."

In the room, he lay down on the bed. As soon as he got comfortable, his phone rang.

"Hello?"

"This is a collect call from China, an inmate at Lowell Correctional Institution. To accept the call, press zero."

Smooth pressed zero.

"This call may be monitored and/or recorded. Thanks for using Securus."

"Hey, baby," China said.

"Hey, boo. Do you miss me?

"Hell yeah. I miss you."

"Well, I'm in Ocala at a hotel. I'll be there to visit you tomorrow. Unfortunately, Gaga and Roxy couldn't make it. They both had to work."

"That's okay. At least I get to see you. How's Roxy's coming along?"

"That place has got the best food I've ever eaten and it stays packed."

"Shit, it's count time. I gotta go. I'll see ya tomorrow, baby."

"I love you."

"I love you, too. Bye."

After putting his phone on the charger, he turned on the T.V. and watched a movie until he fell asleep.

****

Returning to her cell, she saw Rebecca standing at the sink in boxers and a sports bra, drinking a cup of water. She was truly beautiful.

"How was your phone call?" Rebecca asked.

"It was good. Smooth is coming to see me tomorrow."

"Just wish you could come out to the visiting park with me. I bet you and Smooth would like each other. Tomorrow, I'm gonna tell him all about you needing a place to stay and how I want you there."

"Think he's really gonna let me stay there until I get on my feet?"

"Yes. He'll let you stay. Once he sees how beautiful you are, he won't want you to leave."

"China walked over to Rebecca and kissed her on the lips, forcing her tongue into her mouth. Rebecca started to loosen up and kiss back. China slid a hand into Rebecca's boxers and slid a finger into her tight pussy. She was already soaking wet.

"Smooth's gonna love this tight pussy," China told Rebecca, as she pulled Rebecca's boxers off.

China told Rebecca to lie down. As she did so, China got between her legs and started to lick her pussy, spreading open the lips so she could get the tongue inside to tongue-fuck her while rubbing her clit with her thumb. Rebecca's breath turned shallow and she moaned, while thrusting her hips up to meet China's face and fingers. Using her other hand, China slid a finger into Rebecca's ass and started finger fucking her while sucking on her clit. In no time at all, Rebecca exploded all over China's face.

****

"Preston! China Preston! You have a visit," announced the guard over the intercom.

"I'll see you when I get back, Rebecca."

"Okay, hope you have a good visit."

Going downstairs and then outside, China walked toward the visitation park. Once there, she was stripped naked, clothes searched, and then told to get dressed.

After dressing, China went into the visiting area. Looking around, she saw Smooth sitting at a table with a lot of food piled up in front of him. Once he looked up and saw China, he stood up and gave her a big hug and kiss.

"God, I love you so much, China."

"I love you, too, Smooth."

"Well, let's sit down and eat before it gets too cold. Didn't know what you wanted, so I got a little of everything . . . pizza, chicken sandwich, barbeque beef sandwich, Doritos, Fritos, Coke.

"Mmmmm . . . it all sounds good."

China opened the chicken sandwich and removed the bottom bun. She then opened up the pizza and set the top bun and chicken patty on top of the pizza, and then she took a bite.

"Mmmmm . . . Mmmmm. This is so good."

"Glad you like it," Smooth said, opening a bag of Doritos and setting them in front of China.

"Thanks, baby."

"No problem," Smooth replied.

He opened the barbeque beef sandwich and the Fritos. Taking a big bite of the sandwich, Smooth wasn't too sure what to expect. It turned out that it was pretty good.

"We call those sandwiches 18 wheelers. Not sure why, but that's what everyone calls them."

"It's good. So how you doing? They treating you okay?"

"I'm good. And, yes, they are treating me good. Signed up for G.E.D. classes so I can try to get an education . . . and to get GaGa off my back."

"GaGa's right, though. You need to make the best of your time and education is important. What else you do here?"

"I play volleyball. I'm getting pretty good at it, too."

"Volleyball?"

"Yes, volleyball. I love it. It's fun and it's a good workout. What have you been doing?"

"Trying to get that money. My crew keeps growing. Having turf wars with Puerto Ricans. I also bought an apartment building that has six apartments."

"What you gonna do with an apartment building?"

"I'm gonna rent four of them out, and I'm gonna hold two in case something comes up."

"Well, look . . . my girl gets out in about three weeks. She has no friends, no family, and nowhere to go. I told her that she would stay with you in the guest bedroom. Is that okay?"

"Yeah, sure. Just let me know when to expect her."

"Well, you'll need to come pick her up.

"Okay, just let me know when."

"And listen, I've eaten her pussy, and she's eaten mine. I want us three to have a threesome. So if you're interested, you can fuck her. It would make me happy if you two stayed with each other until I got out."

"Let's see how things turn out."

10

After visiting China, Smooth took off for New York. Crossing the Florida-Georgia line, his phone rang.

"Hello?"

"Hey Smooth, it's me, Ronny."

"Waz up, Ronny?"

"I found out where some of those Spanish dudes be hanging out."

"Oh yeah? Where?"

"A spot over in Little Haiti."

"Alright. We will handle it as soon as I get back into town on Monday. Other than that, what's good?"

"Mac called and wants two more of those things."

"Once again, we will handle that once I get back into town."

"Well, see you on Monday then."

As soon as he hung up, the phone rang once more.

"Hello?"

"Waz up, nigga?"

"Hey Banga."

"What's good, Smooth?"

"Nothing. Just finished visiting China. Now I'm on my way to New York."

"Damn, wish I could have come with you. You know . . . to help drive."

"I'm good. If I get tired, I'll pull over. I'm not gonna risk it. When China ran this up, she used to always call me to stay awake."

"Well, bro, if you need to talk, just hit me up."

"I will."

"Nigga, I don't know what you did to Meka, but she can't stop talking about you."

"All I did was talk to her."

"Must have been some hell of a talk," Banga laughed.

"So, what's up? They give you a court date? What's the lawyer saying?"

"Lawyer says he can probably get me a deal for 60 days. If he does, I'll take it, just to get it all over with and get back to Miami."

"Guess I can understand that. How's business doing?"

"This shit is going like hot cakes. The way it's going, I'm gonna need to re-up real soon."

"I will stop by on my way back from New York to drop off a few more."

"Good! While you are here, I want you to meet a few people that just got out of jail and need work. I met them both while I was in, and they both seem to be straight soldiers. And I know you need some people like these two on the team."

"I'll probably be there around dinner time on Monday."

"I'll make sure they're here."

"Well, let me get off here. I'll holla later."

"Later," Banga replied, hanging up.

After a while, Smooth's thoughts turned to China. He loved her to death, but he was scared he was gonna lose her. She and her roommate were lovers and China had feelings for her. Smooth had slept with several women, but no one could compare to China. And Smooth refused to love another woman. Now China wanted her lover to live with them and she wanted Smooth to sleep with her.

Not sure what do, Smooth's mind drifted off onto business. Things had really picked up. Stone now wanted 10 keys; the dude, Mac, wanted two, and he had other customers wanting product. Plus, they were breaking down some for crack and selling that. Altogether, he had about 15 people working the streets for him. Things seemed to be going good. Now, if he could just get rid of the Spanish crew that kept popping up.

****

Pulling up to the security gates outside of El Jefe's house, Smooth waited for a guard to appear. After a few minutes, he finally came out. He wasn't the same guard as last time, but this one was just as big, and he was carrying an MP5 machine gun.

"Can I help you?"

"My name's Smooth and I'm here to see Jefe."

"Is he expecting you?"

"Yes, he is."

"Let me check real fast," he said, as he headed back into the guard shack.

The guard returned a moment later to open the gate and he waved him through. Smooth followed the long twisting driveway all the way up to the house. It always shocked Smooth at how nice and how big Jefe's house was. It was bigger than his entire apartment building.

Pulling up, he was met by two more guards. After getting the money out of his car, Smooth followed them into the library. Setting the money down, Smooth started to look at the books while he waited. Five minutes later, a guard came back in.

"Follow me, please,"

Grabbing the money, he followed the guard outside to the pool, where Jefe was sitting at a table, reading a newspaper.

"Have a seat, my friend," Jefe said, while still reading the paper.

Taking a seat, Smooth took a look around and saw two beautiful women in bikinis by the pool.

"All these school shootings. What is wrong with all these people? Nowhere is safe these days. Denny's, movie theaters, hospitals, schools . . . nowhere is safe!"

"I know, it's like the whole world's going crazy," Smooth said.

"Well, my friend, what can I do for you?"

"I need the regular 30 plus 10 more. Is that okay?"

"Sure."

"Raul!" Jefe yelled.

A minute later, a man showed up and Jefe spoke to him in rapid Spanish. Raul took the money from Smooth and headed back inside.

"You look tired, my friend."

"I am. I drove straight here. Figured I'll get a motel room and rest before I head back to Miami."

"Just be very careful, my friend."

"I will be. By the way, China says hello."

to meet?”

to last time?”

“Yeah, off of 5th Street?”

“Meet me there. Got some people who wanna meet ya.”

“Be there soon.”

A few minutes later, Smooth pulled up to the apartment. He saw Banga, Ham, Meka, and two other guys standing beside a 2015 Dodge Charger, which had been entirely blacked out like a Midnight Edition, and a candy apple red '95 Bubble Chevy Caprice sitting on 28s. Parking beside the blacked-out Charger, Smooth put the car in park, hit the trunk release, and got out of the car. Banga came over with a book bag and handed it to Smooth. After dumping the money into another bag, Smooth put two kilos in Banga's bag and handed it back to him. He then closed the trunk

“All good?” Banga asked.

“Yeah. So who you got cooking that up for ya?”

“My cousin, Ham. You in a hurry?”

“Nah.”

“Good. Come meet my two dawgs.”

Walking over to the group, he noticed Meka looking him up and down. He did the same to her; and just like last time, he thought she was very pretty but just too dark. But right then, he'd take her. Something about her was totally sexy today.

"Breaking his thoughts, he heard Banga tell the two dudes, "This is Smooth. Smooth . . . this is Sue Rabbit and Prince Guru."

"Nice to meet you all."

"I've told them about your little problem with the Spanish people, and they're both ready to help with that and with everything else," Banga informed him.

"Well, as long as you're willing, I could use a few more good men on my team."

"I'm down. Ain't got nothing else to do and I need the money," Guru said.

Smooth looked him over. He was about 6'1" with long dreads.

"Same here, man," Sue chimed in. "Plus I've never been to Miami, so a change in scenery would be nice. How soon you want us to start?"

"As soon as you can."

"Well, why don't we just follow you back down there? Once we find a place to stay and unpack, we will get started."

"Well, I got an empty apartment you can stay at. Its three bedrooms. It's furnished and it's nice."

"Alright, when do we leave?" Guru asked.

"Shit, let's go right now!" Sue responded.

"We will leave in about two hours. I wanna stretch my legs a bit."

"Wanna walk with me, Meka?"

"Sure, where we going?"

"Why don't you choose where we go?"

"If I get to pick, I'd say straight to my bedroom, so I can take you up on that offer."

"What offer?"

"Remember, in the bar before you left, I said I wanted to ride you. Well, I want to."

"So, where do we go?"

"Follow me," she offered, grabbing him and leading him into the apartment and straight to her bedroom.

Once inside, she closed the bedroom door. They started to kiss. Smooth ran his hands down her back and cupped her fat ass. *Damn, this was gonna be fun*, he thought. Breaking away from the kiss, Smooth took off her shirt and noticed that she wasn't wearing a bra. She had small breasts, but they were nice. She reached down and unbuttoned his pants. They fell down around his ankles before he could step out of them, and she pushed him onto the bed. She pulled off her pants and G-string.

Climbing onto the bed, she leaned down and took his dick into her mouth. She sucked it while she was fingering herself. After his dick grew hard, she climbed on top of him and slowly lowered herself onto this hard dick. Leaning forward, she began to kiss him while riding him. Her pussy fit him like a glove.

Within two minutes, she was bucking wildly, making all kinds of moaning noises before she climaxed, Once she came, she stopped. Not having cum yet himself, Smooth grabbed her and rolled over so he was on top. He started slowly sliding his cock almost all the way in and then out, and then slamming it back in. When he felt he was getting close, he stopped.

"Get on your hands and knees."

She did as she was told.

"Damn, you got a fat ass!"

He slid his dick back in. Sliding in and out, he watched his cock stretch out her pussy. Faster and faster. As soon as he was about to cum, he pulled out and shot his load all over her ass.

****

"Hell of a way to stretch your legs," Banga said.

"You're just jealous!"

"Yeah, of you and my cousin."

"I know you Stuart boys . . . inbred!"

"Fuck you, nigga!" Banga laughed.

Looking at Sue and Guru, Smooth asked, "You two ready to go?"

"Yep," Guru replied.

"Hell yeah. Can't wait to get out of Martin County," Sue said.

"All right, Banga. I'll see ya on the next trip."

"Y'all drive safe and be careful," Banga said.

Sue got in the Caprice and Guru got in the blacked-out Charger. Smooth led the way in his Audi A4. Before leaving Stuart, they stopped to fill up their tanks and get something to eat. Then they got on the highway.

****

Pulling up to the duplex on 33rd Street, Smooth looked around. Seeing nothing out of place, he got out of his car. After parking, Sue and Guru came over. They all headed up the steps on Ronny's side and knocked on his door. Several seconds later, Ronny opened the door.

"Hey, bro. Come on in," Ronny said, stepping back so the three guys could enter.

"How was your trip?"

"Good. How's things up here?"

"Good, but we are low. Need to re-up."

"I'll have it ready for tomorrow at lunch time."

"Anyhow! Ronny, this is Sue and Guru. Guys . . . this is my right-hand man, Ronny."

"What's up?" Sue said.

"How ya doing?" Guru asked.

"Ronny, these two are gonna help with the Spanish problem and with sales."

"When we gonna hit these damn Mexicans?" Ronny asked.

"Well, why not hit them tonight?" Smooth suggested.

"How we gonna do it?" Ronny inquired.

"We take two stolen cars with three or four men in each. Drive up, pop out, and fire up the whole place. Then get out of there. Real simple," Smooth said.

"Alright, what kind of guns?" Ronny asked.

"Well, I have a few AKs and assault rifles in my trunk," Sue said.

"What . . . you just carry that stuff around?" Guru asked.

"Hell yeah. Never know when you're gonna need to go to war. Always be prepared!"

"How many blocks we holding down?" Smooth asked.

"About 20."

"That's good, but after tonight, I want at least 10 more. My goal is to hold down the whole east side."

"We arc on our way, slowly but surely."

"Alright, let's get together tonight at about 8:00 p.m."

"We meet up here. I'll have the cars and the men ready," Ronny said.

"I'll have the guns," Sue said.

"Okay, let me show you boys where the apartments are and then I need to leave and handle some business.

Once at the apartments, Smooth showed them the locks and the way to use them. He set it up so every time someone approached the door, a picture would be taken and sent to all three phones. This was just in case one of them wasn't answering.

"You all like it?" Smooth asked.

"Hell yeah!" Guru answered.

"Compared to where we just came from, this is a palace," Sue said.

"And the beds are a lot softer," Smooth said, with a laugh.

"Alright, you two get settled in. Remember, 8:00 p.m. tonight."

Heading out the door, Smooth pulled out his phone and dialed up Amanda.

"Hello?" she answered on the second ring.

"Hey, it's Smooth. I need your help again."

"You know where I live, so come on by and bring about four boxes of baking soda."

****

Pulling up to Amanda's apartment complex, Smooth put the car in park. Looking around, he saw nothing strange, and he didn't see anyone else around. He popped the trunk, grabbed the bag with the baking soda from the back seat, and walked around and opened the trunk. Unzipping one of the duffle bags, he pulled out two kilos and put them in the bag, along with the baking soda. He then grabbed the bag and slammed the trunk.

Once at Amanda's door, he knocked three times and waited. A few moments later, the door opened and Amanda let him in. Smooth went straight to the kitchen after shutting and locking the front door. Amanda followed. Upon entering the kitchen, she walked up to Smooth, put her arms around his neck, and kissed him.

A few seconds later, she asked, "What's wrong?"

"Nothing, why?"

"You just seem really tense."

"Got a bit of a headache and having problems with another crew over turf."

"Come on, follow me," she said, as she took off for another room.

Wearing tight shorts, which really showed off her beautiful ass, and a belly shirt, he couldn't help but follow her. Opening the door on the left, she left it opened for him to follow. Inside was not what he expected. There was a full-size bed with a canopy, pink walls, and stuffed animals everywhere. Definitely a girl's room.

"Alright, mister, strip naked and lay on the bed."

He slowly took off his clothes as he watched her strip out of her clothes. After stripping, he lay down on his back.

"Nope, turn over. On your stomach."

Once he flipped over, she straddled him. Smooth then felt some type of liquid pour over his back. Then she slowly rubbed the lotion all over his back. Once that was done, she started to massage him gently. Feeling her hands all over his body was turning him on. He could feel himself getting hard as a rock.

"You know, this is really turning me on."

"Oh really?"

"Yeah, really!"

"Would you like me to fix that for you?"

"I'd love you to."

"Turn over," she said, getting off his back.

He flipped over onto his back. His hard dick was sticking straight up. She straddled him again and slowly slid her tight pussy down over his hard cock.

"Ahhh . . . this is so good. Do you like it like this?" she asked, as she slowly rode his dick.

"Hell, yeah! Feels amazing!"

She slowly rode up and down. He looked down and watched his massive cock disappear into her hot, tight pussy. Then he looked up and watched her breasts bounce up and down in rhythm to her riding his cock.

"Hmmmm . . . don't know how much more of this I can take before I cum," Smooth exclaimed.

Instead of answering, she sped up, riding him faster. Smooth closed his eyes as he tried his best to hold back. Smooth noticed a chance in her breathing. It was coming in gasps and he swore her pussy tightened. She moaned loudly and screamed out in ecstasy as she came. Feeling her pussy spasm sent him over the edge. He exploded and came deep in her womb.

"Thanks! I really needed that," Smooth said.

"I did, too. So we're even."

Getting dressed, Amanda asked him not to put on his shirt yet. She then went over to the closet and dug around for a minute before returning.

"Here, I want you to wear these at all times."

"A bulletproof vest? Where did you get it?"

"I bought it online for my ex, but didn't get a chance to give it to him before he was gunned down."

"Thanks!"

"Just make sure you always wear it, okay?"

"Don't worry. I will wear it."

"You better!"

****

Pulling up to the duplex on 33rd Street, Smooth saw cars everywhere. Both driveways and the yards were packed. He parked in the street and walked up the side that Ronny lived on. Before he could knock, the door was opened by Ronny.

"About time you showed up."

"Hey, I got lost, okay?" Smooth laughed.

"Everyone else is here."

Inside, Smooth saw eight people: Neko, Bobby, Sue, Guru, Ronny, and three others.

"Alright, everybody listen up!"

After everybody stopped talking, Ronny continued.

"We got an older Aerostar minivan and an older Chevy pick-up. The plan is to have two or three of you all lay in the bed of the truck; and once we get there, you all pop up and unload on thie. At the same time, we will have three in the van, two in back, and one in the passenger side. Once we pull up, you roll the side door open and unload on them. Real simple. In and out in no time. We will all meet back here. Any questions? None? Alright, good. Now, Sue, what have you got for us?"

In response, Sue grabbed two long duffle bags off the floor and put them on the table. Opening the first one, he pulled out two AKs with 30-round clips. He handed one to Ronny and one to Bobby. He then reached back into the bag and pulled out a Tech 9mm and an Uzi. After everyone got their guns except for Smooth, Sue reached in the bag and grabbed a wicked gun.

"What the hell is this?" Smooth asked.

"This, my friend, is a Colt 556 assault rifle."

"What does it matter as long as it shoots?" Neko said.

"Are you sure all these work?" Ronny asked.

"I've tested each gun personally and fired them all. Believe me, they all work."

"Alright, let's head out then."

111

They all headed out to the van and truck.

Smooth went to the truck and climbed in the back with Sue and Bobby.

"Well, it's rock 'n' roll time, boys!" one of the new dudes said.

"Listen, when we get there, I'm gonna bang on the back windows. As soon as you hear me bang, pop up and let them have it."

Smooth, Sue, and Bobby all lay down in the bed of the truck and tried to get as comfortable as possible for the ride over to little Haiti.

"You ready for this?" Smooth asked Bobby.

"Yeah, I'm ready."

After what seemed like an eternity, they felt the truck slowing, and then they heard the driver bang on the window. Smooth sat up quickly and took a quick look. There was a little restaurant with indoor-outdoor seating. Everything looked full. Without hesitation, he pulled out his gun and opened fire. Tat! Tat! Tat! Tat! Tat! Tat! At the same time, he saw Bobby opening it up. Bang! Bang! Bang! He heard what sounded like a war zone. BOOM! Tat! Tat! Chop! Chop! Bang! Bang!

Bodies were everywhere. People were tripping on the others, trying to escape. Smooth aimed at the ones trying to escape. Finally, his gun ran dry. He was empty with no spare clips. Smooth banged on the window and told the driver to go. Smooth, Bobby, and Sue all lay back down for the drive back.

"We really got those damn Mexicans," Bobby said.

"Yeah, we got 'em," Sue replied.

Before they knew it, they were back at the duplex.

112

"You all get out so I can go dump this truck," the driver said.

After they got out and watched the truck disappear, they saw the minivan pull up. Ronny, Guru, and Neko got out and the minivan pulled off.

Once back inside, Ronny said, "We did it!"

They all started slapping each other's back and acting as if they just won a football game.

"Alright, what should we do with the guns?" Smooth asked.

"Just keep them in case you need them again. I can easily get more, no problem," Sue said.

"Okay, I got to get going," Guru said. "When do you want us back over here?"

"Be here about 1:00 p.m. and we will have some work," Smooth said.

"Like what?"

"Remember, Mac wanted two of those."

"Oh yeah. I got it in the car. You wanna go over there now?"

"We can."

"Well, let's go."

"Alright, everybody out. We got to go handle some business."

Everyone piled out the doors. Smooth and Ronny got into his Audi A4 and cranked up the music. Some hard rock for the bass. Disturbed's *The Light* was blasting out the speakers.

As they reached Club Rage, they noticed the line was all the way around the building. Luckily for them, they didn't have to wait in line. On the way over, Ronny called Mac to let him know they were on their way. Mac instructed them to use the private entrance.

Parking in the back, Smooth took a look around. Seeing no threat, he popped open the trunk. Walking to the back of the car, Smooth opened the trunk and pulled out a bag with the two keys in it. He then closed the trunk and headed to the back door. Once they were at the back door, Ronny used his cell phone to let Mac knew they were there.

A few minutes later, the back door opened. As it opened, Smooth saw two bouncers, both were about 6'5" and weighed at least 300 pounds. They both had bulging muscles. Definitely not the type you'd want to pick a fight with.

Once inside, they were led upstairs to the same office as last time. One of the bouncers knocked on the door and then opened it for Ronny and Smooth to enter. After they entered, the bouncer closed the door, leaving just Mac, Smooth, and Ronny inside the room. Mac was sitting behind a desk; but as they entered, Mac stood up and walked around the desk to shake their hands.

"A please seeing you two. Can I get you gentlemen anything to drink?"

"Rum would be nice," Smooth said.

He was getting to really enjoy rum and the way it made it feel.

"I'll take some Fireball, if you have it," Ronny asked.

Mac went over to a built-in bar and poured the drinks. Then he brought them back over to the guys.

"Are you two planning on staying and having a good time, or are you leaving after our business is completed?"

"I'll be staying to get my party on," Ronny answered.

"I'll also be staying," Smooth agreed.

"Good. I will have you both sit in the V.I.P. section. Anything you need, just ask."

"Okay," Smooth said.

"Now to business. You have the two keys?"

"Yep! Here you go," Smooth replied, handing the bag to Mac.

"Well, here is your money," Mac said, giving him a bag in return.

"Listen, I know I've been getting only two keys, but I want to start getting five. Is that a possibility?"

"Yeah, we can handle that. Just call us when you are ready to re-up," Smooth said.

"Alright, then you two gentlemen have fun."

Leaving the office, Smooth told the bouncer, "I need to take this to the car, and I'll be right back."

"I'll hold the door open for you," the bouncer replied.

"I'll be in V.I.P. waiting on you."

Smooth ran out to the car, put the bag in the trunk, and returned to the club and went straight to the V.I.P. section.

As soon as he stepped into the V.I.P. section, a server asked him if he'd like a drink.

"Rum and Coke."

"Is that all?"

"Nah, better yet, just give me a bottle of rum."

"I'll be right back."

Ronny hadn't even been in the club for five minutes and he already had a girl sitting on his lap. Looking around, Smooth saw hot bitches everywhere. One little redbone in a while dress caught his attention.

When the server returned with this bottle of rum, he said, "See that girl in the white dress?"

"Yeah, I see her."

"Will you ask her if she'd like to join me in V.I.P.?"

"Sure," the server replied while walking away.

Smooth watched the server make her way through the crowd to the girl in the white dress. Once she reached her, she leaned up close to give her the message. Then she leaned away and pointed toward Smooth. When the girl looked up at him, he waved at her. She smiled and gave a little wave back. Then she started to make her way over to the V.I.P. section. Smooth watched her the whole time.

When she arrived, Smooth asked, "Would you like a drink?"

"Sure, double Crown," Smooth told the server, who headed to get the drink.

"V.I.P., huh? Are you like famous or something?"

"No, but the owner is a friend, so he be looking out for me."

"That's cool! This is my first time in this club . . . and my first time ever in V.I.P."

About that time, the server returned with her drink.

"Well, let's toast to a night of first," Smooth said, holding the bottle of rum out to toast. She clinked glasses with his.

"To a night of first," she said.

"So what's your name, shorty?"

"Just call me Missy."

"Well, just call me Missy, I'm Smooth, and it is very nice to meet you."

"Same here. Oh, come on, let's dance!" she suggested, as she set her glass down on the table. "This is one of my favorite songs," she said, as Selena Gomez's *Same Old Love* came out pounding through the speakers.

Smooth set down his bottle of rum, grabbed her, and started to dance. Shorty knew how to bump and grind. Just dancing with her was making him hard. She had to have felt his erection though his Giorgio Armani slacks.

Sure enough, she turned around to face him and leaned in.

"Did I do that?" she asked, as she grabbed his dick through his pants.

"Hell, yeah, you did that," he announced.

"Well, let's go sit down and take a break," she said, leading him over to the couch.

Once he sat down, she bent over him and undid his pants, reached in, and pulled out his erection. Then she pulled up her dress and straddled him. She slowly lowered herself onto him. He felt her tight walls gripping his cock, as she went up and down slowly.

"Do you like this?"

"Yeah" was all he could say.

"I've never done it in public before; but remember, tonight's a night of firsts!" she said.

Smooth kept looking around, worried someone was watching. But this pussy felt so good, he didn't care who was watching, as long as no one tried to stop them. She was looking him in the eye as she rode him up and down. Feeling his balls tighten and knowing he was fixing to cum, he lifted up trying to meet her thrust for thrust. Suddenly, he climaxed and his whole body went rigid, as he came inside her. But she didn't stop. She picked up her pace. She put her face in the nape of his neck. He heard her moan and begin to breathe heavy, until he finally felt her cum. Unable to speak yet, she just sat there. After a few moments, she stood up, grabbed her drink, and sat down beside him.

"Oh my God! I can't believe we just did that!" she said.

"Well, believe it!" he laughed.

"God, you must think I'm some kind of whore."

"I didn't say that."

"No, but that's what you're probably thinking, but I promise I've never done anything like this before. I've always wanted to try it, but never had the chance."

"Well, did you enjoy it?'

"It was like totally fantastic!"

"Fantastic, huh?"

"Yeah!"

"Well, Missy, what do you do for a living?"

"I'm a nurse for hospice."

"Do you like it?"

"Sometimes, but it can be emotionally taxing."

"What ya mean?" Smooth asked.

"Do you know what hospice is?"

"Not really."

"Well, it's where a nurse takes care of a patient during his or her last days. So basically, all of my patients die; and it can be very depressing, especially if you grow fond of them."

"Yeah, I don't think I could do that. You're stronger than I am."

"It takes a lot out of you, especially when you have been taking care of a patient who has no family or friends. They get so lonely. If I have a patient who doesn't have anyone left, I try to spend a lot of time with them. Those are the ones who really get to me."

"That must suck! Why do you keep doing it?"

"Well, somebody's got to do it, right?"

"Yeah, I guess so. But I could never do it."

"So what do you do for a living, mister?"

"I own a few rental properties."

"Must be nice," she laughed.

"Yeah, it's nice to be able to sleep in. No 9-to-5 shit."

"Hey, I'm hungry. That good dick of yours got me an appetite. Let's go get some food."

"Let me tell my dawg I'm leaving and then we can go."

Looking around, Smooth finally spotted Ronny. He walked up to him.

"Bro, I'm fixing to get out of here. You need a ride?"

"Nah, have fun and be careful."

****

Being so late, there were very few restaurants from which to choose. Finally, the picked Denny's.

"Thank God for Denny's," she joked.

"Yeah, right. Always open and their food's pretty good."

"Especially their biscuits and gravy."

Once inside, they got a table in the back. A waitress appeared and asked, "What would you like to drink?"

"Sprite," Missy replied.

"Coke, no ice please."

"Be right back."

She returned with their drinks.

"Are you ready to order or do you need more time?"

"I'll take four biscuits and two things of gravy."

"Give me the chicken sampler, please."

"Alright, is that all?"

"Yes, ma'am," Smooth answered.

After the waitress left, Missy said, "I don't understand it."

"Understand what?"

"They sell biscuits and they sell gravy, but they don't sell biscuits and gravy together. You got to buy them separately and then pour the gravy on the biscuits yourself. It honestly makes no sense."

"You're right, it makes no sense. They probably do it just to drive people like you crazy."

"You might be right," she laughed.

Missy had a nice laugh, and Smooth enjoyed listening to it.

"I still can't believe we had sex inside a night club with all those people around. But I think knowing all those people were around us made the sex even better."

"It was pretty good," Smooth laughed.

"What are you laughing at?"

"Just had an image of us doing it right here on the table."

"Sounds like fun. Want to try it?"

Before Smooth could reply, she said, "Just joking, but maybe we can try it in the bathroom."

"Yeah right."

"Serious. I'm not joking. I'm going to the bathroom. Give me two minutes and then follow me, alright?" she asked.

"Okay."

She got up and walked toward the bathroom.

Damn, she got a sexy walk, Smooth thought.

After two minutes, Smooth stood up, looked around to make sure no one was looking, and then headed to the bathroom.

Fuck! I can't believe I'm doing this! Smooth thought.

After one last look around, he opened the door to the women's bathroom and stepped inside, closing the door behind him. Looking back at the door, he saw no lock, so anyone could walk in at any time. But he didn't care. He just wanted more of that good pussy. When he walked up to her, she got on her knees, unzipped his pants, reached into his boxers, and pulled out his dick. She put it in her mouth and went to town until he was hard. Once he had an erection, she stood up, turned around, lifted up her dress, and bent over the sink. Smooth stepped up and slowly slid his hard cock into her hot, wet pussy. Her walls gripped him like a glove. He couldn't handle much more of her tight pussy, so he reached around and played with her clit while he fucked her. It took coordination but he managed.

Within three minutes, she started to breathe heavily and her knees started to buckle as she came. Smooth kept going until he came a minute later. As he pulled out and zipped his pants back up, someone opened the door.

An older lady stepped inside.

"Oh my, I'm sorry," she replied, as she went to turn around.

"Don't be sorry. We were just leaving," Smooth said.

Smooth and Missy both walked past the old lady and they burst out laughing.

Heading back to their table, they finished their meal, paid the bill, and headed back to her house.

****

The next morning, Smooth headed over to Amanda's. After knocking twice on the door, she opened the door. She stood there in a bath towel looking really tired.

"Sorry to wake you up. Do I need to come back later?"

"Nah, come on in. I just started a pot of coffee. Once I get a few cups in me, I'll be fine."

"Stay up late partying?" Smooth asked.

"Nope. I stayed up late bagging all this just for you. I haven't been out to party in months."

"Can't stay cooped up. Gotta get out and enjoy life."

"Yeah, yeah!"

Walking over to the coffee pot, she poured herself a cup and asked, 'You want a cup?"

"No, but some water would be nice."

She grabbed a glass, filled it up with water, and handed it to him. "Thanks."

"No problem."

"Not today, but probably in two or three days, I'm gonna need you to cook up two or three more keys."

"Hey, as long as you're paying, I don't mind. Trying to save up enough to retire early," she laughed.

"Me, too. I don't want to live like this forever. I want to settle down, go legit, and live a good life."

"Me, too. I figure after I save up some and find a good man; maybe I'll have a few kids and enjoy the American dream."

"Sounds like a fairy tale to me."

"I just want to be happy."

"I can understand that, but just don't getting your hopes up!"

"I won't! Believe me."

"Well, I hate to be rude, but I gotta go."

"I'll stop back by in a few days."

"Okay, I'll see ya then."

11

China sat at the table watching the news, worried to death about Smooth. Once again, the news lady repeats herself:

"I'm here live where there was a mass shooting last night that seems to be gang-related. Eyewitnesses said two vehicles, a blue minivan, and a red pick-up truck, pulled up outside this restaurant and several black males popped out and started shooting. So far, there are 16 dead and nine injured, three of whom are in critical condition and might not make it. If you have any information about this shooting, the police ask that you please call them immediately."

"China," she heard her name and turned to see a girl by the phone calling out her name. "China, it's your turn for the phone."

China got up, went to the phone, and dialed Smooth's number. After getting no answer, she called Roxy.

"Hello?"

"This is a collect call from China, an inmate at Lowell Correctional Institution. To accept the call, press zero."

Roxy pressed zero.

"This call may be monitored and/or recorded. Thanks for using Securus."

"God, I hate that automated shit," Roxy said.

"Yeah, me, too!"

"So, have you heard from Smooth lately?"

"Yeah, he ate dinner at my restaurant last night."

"I just called him and got no answer."

"Do you want me to give him a message?"

"Just tell him that I love him and let him know that I mailed him a letter this morning."

"I'll let him know as soon as I talk to him."

"So, how's the restaurant business?"

"Busy! Very busy! I got tables booked a month ahead of time. It's totally crazy. I never expected it to take off like this. It's a dream come true, thanks to you and Smooth."

After a few more minutes, the automated voice announced, "You have one minute remaining."

"Well, I'm glad you called. I love you and will see you next weekend. But call me again in a few days," Roxy said.

"I will and I love you too. Bye."

"NEXT ON THE PHONE," China yelled, as she headed to her room to finish reading Silk White's *Married to Da Streets*.

****

Pulling up to Ronny's, Smooth saw a 15' blacked-out Dodge Charger and a candy apple- red '95 Chevy Caprice sitting out front, which meant that Sue Rabbit and Prince Guru were already there. Parking in the street, Smooth looked around and saw nobody outside or sitting in cars. Nothing appeared strange, so he popped open the trunk, grabbed the bag with the cooked-up coke, and headed to Ronny's door, where he knocked twice. It was opened almost immediately by Ronny

"Come on in and join the party," Ronny said.

Once inside, Smooth saw Guru and Sue standing at the table with several handguns on it.

"What's this, a war council?" Smooth joked.

"Nah, but I brought some toys you'd probably like to have," Sue said. "As a matter of fact, this one's for you," Sue continued, handing Smooth a pistol.

"What is it?" Smooth asked.

"It's an FN Five Seven pistol. It carries 20 5.7 x 28mm armor-piercing rounds. Guaranteed to stop anything short of a tank," Sue said.

"How much?" Smooth asked.

"It's on the house this time," Sue said.

"Thanks! Ronny . . . here is more product," Smooth said, handing Ronny the backpack.

"Be right back," Ronny answered, as he exited into the other room.

A few minutes later, he returned and handed Smooth the same backpack.

"Here's the money. Everybody already got theirs?"

"Good, good!"

"So what's the plan?" Guru asked Smooth.

"What do ya mean?"

"Well, do we continue to slump these fucking wetbacks, or do we start worrying about setting our boundaries?"

"Let's just wait and see what they decided to do," Smooth answered.

"Anything else while I'm here?" Smooth asked.

"Nope. We good. We will call if we need ya's."

"Alright, later," Smooth said, as he headed back to his car.

****

The dashboard clock read 4:37 p.m. Smooth figured he might as well enjoy an early dinner. With that in mind, he headed towards Roxy's. Just like last time, the place was almost packed.

Before the waitress could tell him they were full, Smooth told her, "My name's Smooth. I have a reserved table."

"Oh, yes, of course. Follow me," she said, before turning and heading to his table. Once Smooth sat down, she handed him a menu.

"What can I get you to drink?"

"A Coke. No ice, please. And if you see Roxy, please let her know that I'm here."

"Sure thing."

Off she went to get his drink. Watching her walk away, Smooth noticed she had a mean walk. But in the face, she looked like a pit bull. Smooth was enjoying sleeping with all the girls, but he couldn't wait for China to get out. Screwing all those women might be fun, but nothing and no one could come close to China. He couldn't wait to visit her that weekend.

"Here's your drink, sir. Are you ready to order?" she inquired, breaking his train of thought.

"Yes, I'll have the boneless pork chops, mashed potatoes, and dinner rolls."

"Is that all?"

"Well, go ahead and give me some macaroni and cheese, too."

"Alright, I'll be back with your food in a little bit," she said, walking away.

Yep, definitely has a sexy walk. Might be fuckable from the back, but face to face is out of there, he thought.

"Hey stranger!" Roxy said, sliding into the booth across from Smooth.

"Hey Roxy! Full house again, huh?"

"Yeah. It's crazy, huh? Never imagined business would be so good. The food critics gave me five stars. How awesome is that?"

"The food is definitely five starts. Everything I've had to eat here has been busting. Whoever you got cooking really knows what they're doing."

"China called me last night. She said she tried to call you but you didn't answer. She says she loves you and will call tonight. So make sure you answer."

"Okay."

"Are you going to visit her this weekend?"

"Yeah, I'm gonna see her Saturday."

"I can't go this week, but next week I'm gonna go see her."

"Just let me know and we will go together."

"Okay. Well, I hate to be rude, but I got to get back to work. Enjoy your food," Roxy said.

As she walked away, the waitress came over with his dinner and set it down in front of him.

"Enjoy your meal. If you need something else, just let me know."

"Okay."

As she walked away, Smooth dug into his food. And like all the other meals he had eaten at Roxy's, it was off the chain.

While eating, his phone rang. Looking at the display, he didn't recognize the number.

"Hello?" he answered.

"Yes, mon. Can I speak to Smooth?"

"Hey Stone. It's me."

"Hey mon. How ya doin'?"

"I'm good, Stone. What ya need?"

"Umm, I need like 10 of dos tings as soon as possible. Will dat be a problem?"

"No, no problem. Meet me at the gas station at 1:00 p.m. tomorrow."

"Okay, mon. Tanks!"

Smooth hung up and continued to eat his meal. After he finished, he set a $20 on the table, paid his bill, and headed to this car.

****

When he arrived back at his apartment building, he pushed the elevator button for Miranda's floor, figuring he might as well visit her and pick up Zorro. Once he got off the elevator, he knocked on her door. As soon as he knocked, he heard Zorro barking with excitement. Miranda opened the door and Zorro began jumping up on Smooth, standing on his back legs with his front legs on Smooth's chest.

"Looks like somebody missed you."

129

"God, he's getting big," Smooth said.

"Come on in," Miranda said, as she turned and headed to her kitchen. Smooth followed with Zorro at his heels. "Can I get you something to drink?"

"Some rum would be nice."

She reached into a cabinet and pulled out a bottle of rum. Filling up a glass to the top, she handed it to him.

"So, how was your trip?"

"It was good."

"Well, I rented three of your apartments while you were out of town."

"Thanks. I got a few friends staying in apartment five."

"Good, almost a full house."

Smooth looked Miranda up and down. She was wearing a skirt and spaghetti-strap blouse. She looked good. Smooth set his drink down, stood up, and stood next to her. Without another word, he leaned into her and kissed her. When he felt her start to kiss back, his hand grabbed her ass. He could never get over how fat her ass was. He turned her around and started kissing her neck while playing with her breasts. He felt her nipples getting hard as a rock. He bent her over, pulled her skirt up, and pulled her panties to the side. With that done, he undid his pants and pulled out his erection. He put his cock against her waiting pussy, shoving his whole cock into her in one smooth thrust. Hearing her gasp really turned him on. Smooth started thrusting in and out, listening to Miranda's moans while she threw her ass back. In no time she came. After she came, she told him to stop.

"But I haven't cum yet," he pleaded.

"I know. I'll be right back."

Less than a minute later, she returned with a bottle of KY jelly. After getting ready, she bent back over the table, reached behind her to grab Smooth's cock, and guided it into her tight ass. Smooth slowly slid in and out enjoying the feel of her tight ass. Feeling himself about to cum, he sped up until he finally busted a nut inside her ass.

After catching her breath, Miranda said, "Let me go wash up. I'll be right back."

While she went to the bathroom, Smooth sat at the table, finished his drink, and petted Zorro. Five minutes later, Miranda returned to the kitchen. Without even asking, Miranda grabbed the bottle of rum and refilled his glass. She then poured herself one and sat down at the table alongside Smooth.

"I got another apartment building you might like. It just came up for sale today. Would you be interested?" she asked.

"Yeah, I'll take a look at it."

"It's a little more expensive, but there are 10 apartments. It's pretty nice."

"When can I come by and look at it?"

"Come by about lunch time and we will do it then, because I'm busy all afternoon tomorrow."

"So about noon?"

"Yeah, that sounds good. Maybe we can have lunch while you're there."

"How about I bring lunch with me?"

"Sounds good."

"Well, I hate to go, but I got things I need to handle."

"No problem. I'll see you tomorrow."

Grabbing Zorro's leash and attaching it to his collar, Smooth went outside to let Zorro handle his business. He then headed up to his apartment. As he was unlocking the door, his phone rang. He closed the door behind him, took Zorro's leash off, and then answered the phone without checking the display.

"Hello?"

"This is a collect call from China, an inmate at Lowell Correctional Institution. To accept the call, press zero."

Smooth pressed zero.

"This call may be monitored and/or recorded. Thank you for using Securus."

"Hey beautiful, Smooth said.

"Well, hey handsome," China replied.

"Sorry I missed your call last night. I was busy and had my phone turned off. I ate at Roxy's tonight and she gave me your message."

"So, are you coming up this week?"

"Yeah. I'll be there to see you on Saturday."

"Listen, they got this new thing where friends and family can place orders for us. A little care package thing. It's mycarepack.com. Think you can order something for me?"

"Sure. I'll go see Roxy tomorrow, and we can both sit down and order you a care package."

"I'd really appreciate it."

"God, I can't wait to see you and hug you."

"You have one minute left," announced the automated voice.

"Well, I love you and will call again tomorrow night."

"Alright. I love you. Bye."

****

Passing the gas station, Smooth slowed down and looked around. Stone was in his usual place, leaning against his car. Smooth continued circling the block to make sure nothing was out of place and that no one was watching or paying attention. After circling around the block once more, Smooth pulled up alongside Stone. Smooth looked around one more time and then popped the trunk. Getting out of the car, he went around to the back and met Stone.

"Hey mon. Was starting to think you forgot."

"No, just had some other business. Sorry to make you wait."

"No problem, mon. Here's your money, mon," Stone said, handing Smooth a backpack.

"Here's your stuff," Smooth replied, handing Stone a duffle bag.

"Dis be some good shit, mon. It sells fast. Know what I mean, mon?"

"Yeah, it's good 'cause it's pure coke."

"Well, I'll see you again in a few weeks, mon."

"Alright, drive careful."

After getting back in his car and pulling away, he headed to Roxy's. On his way, he replayed his "lunch" with Miranda over in his head. He showed up with a large pizza. After eating and watching the video of the new apartment building, he decided to buy it. Then he and Miranda had wild sex on her office desk, knowing the receptionist heard the whole thing.

****

Pulling into Roxy's, he grabbed his laptop and went inside. The same waitress from the day before was working, and she took him straight to his table.

"Same as yesterday? Coke, no ice?" she asked.

"Yes, please, and would you let Roxy know that I need to see her."

"Of course."

She headed off to the back. A second later, Roxy came out with his Coke.

"Hey Smooth."

"Hey. I need you for a few minutes. Sit over here with me so you can see the screen."

"What are you looking at?" Roxy asked, as she slid in next to him.

"They got this new thing where we can send China a care package. Thought you'd like to help me order one for her."

"You guessed right."

When the screen showed up, they started reading, "Hmm . . . Pop Tarts, peanut butter cookies, Doritos, Fritos . . . all kinds of stuff she'd like."

"How about this chili? And Tostitos?"

"Yeah, she should like that. Let's get her some pork rinds, too."

"What about cookies? Peanut butter chocolate cream, lemon cream, vanilla cream, or chocolate chip?"

"Let's order her three of each, just to be sure."

Twenty minutes later, they had finished up the order.

"Well, now that that's done, I need to get back to work."

"How's GaGa doing?"

"She's doing well. She's been doing a lot of overtime. She even came in here and helped a few times."

"Is she gonna visit China with us . . . not this week but next week?"

"Don't know, but I will ask her."

"Alright, I'll let you get back to work."

Grabbing his laptop, he headed out to his car. After setting it in the back seat, he got in the car and headed to Ronny's.

****

As he pulled up the duplex, he saw Ronny about to get inside the driver's seat of a new Lexus RX350 F sport.

"Whose car you steal?" Smooth joked, as he got out of the car.

"Nobody's, nigga! This my new ride," Ronny answered, with pride in his voice.

"It's nice. How much you pay?"

"I put down $5,000 and got to pay $350 a month."

"That's not bad. So where you heading?"

"Was going to check on a few of our spots. Wanna come along?"

"Yeah, sure."

"Climb in. I'll drive."

Once they were in the Lexus, Ronny pulled out of the driveway. "Bitch got a bad-ass sound system, too." Ronny said, turning the radio on and turning it up, as Chris Brown's *Back to Sleep* came on.

After a few blocks, they pulled up to a liquor store where Sue Rabbit's red Caprice was sitting. Leaning against the car were Sue, Prince Guru, and Eddie, one of the new guys. Sue Rabbit's stereo was turned up playing Travis Scott's *Antidote*. Getting out of the Lexus, Ronny, and Smooth gave Sue Rabbit, Prince Guru, and Eddie some dap. A few seconds later, a white Toyota Avalon pulled into the lot. Eddie went over to take care of the customer.

"Well, how's business going?" Smooth asked.

"Fast. Every time we turn around, another crackhead is pulling up. Had a police officer trying to cause problems, but we gave him $1,000. He said if we gave him $1,000 every few weeks, he'd keep everyone off of us. And since he's a sergeant, he's got some pull. So I figured it's best to just pay him."

"You did the right thing. Other than that, how's things going?"

"Good."

"Alright. Well, we gonna go and check on a few more spots. We will get up with ya later."

Getting back into the Lexus, Ronny turned up the radio to *Hotline Bling* by Drake.

"Got to stop and get some gas," Ronny said.

"Cool."

Parking at the gas pump, Smooth said, "I'll go in and pay and get us some drinks, while you pump the gas. What you want to drink?"

"Just get me a Pepsi."

"Okay," Smooth answered and walked into the store. Grabbing their drinks, he walked up to the counter where an attractive blonde was working.

"Is this all?"

"No, I need $20 on pump three."

'That will be $23.75, sir."

Smooth handed her a $50 bill, adding, "Keep the change."

As Smooth walked out of the store, he heard a car slam on its brakes. Looking up, he saw a black Honda with a Spanish guy holding an AK47 pointed at him. But before he could even blink . . . Tat! Tat! Tat! . . . Smooth caught four bullets to the chest. He hit the ground hard. He heard what sounded like a gunfight before he passed out.

****

"What ya doing, China?" Rebecca asked, as she walked into the cell.

"Thinking."

"About what?"

"About Smooth."

"What about Smooth?"

"Well, see, I told him about us being lovers. I also told him that if he had sexual needs, he could sleep with someone since I wasn't there to take care of his desires."

"Okay, so what's the problem?"

"I'm worried that he might fall in love with someone else."

"Do you really think he could do that?"

"I don't know. I lost my virginity to him and we've been through a lot. He's the only boyfriend I've had. Me and him have been through some hard times, but our love's always held."

"Then it will hold through this, too."

"I sure hope you're right."

"Plus, I get out in three weeks. I'll be there to make sure he don't fall in love with anyone else."

"Yeah, that's true. I can't wait to see how you all are gonna get along. I think you two will have a lot of fun together."

"I can't wait to have some fun. It's been a long five years."

"I bet it has."

"Hopefully, your three years go by fast."

"So far, it's going by fast, but that's because I have you here to help me. I'm really gonna miss you."

"I'm gonna miss you, too."

****

Coming to, Smooth lay there trying to catch his breath and feeling as if he had been hit in the chest with a sledgehammer—as well as the back of his head. He remembered being shot . . . and then blackness. Smooth finally felt someone touching him. Opening his eyes, he saw the pure horror and panic on Ronny's face, as he felt Smooth's chest for bullet wounds.

"A bulletproof vest? You lucky son of a bitch! Come on get up. We got to get out of here before the police show up."

"Help me," Smooth gasped.

With Ronny's help, Smooth was able to get up and get into the Lexus. After they took off and left the gas station, Smooth said, "I think I broke a rib or two."

"Nah, probably just bruised them. Damn, you had me worried. I saw you get hit and go down. I pulled my ratchet and unloaded on those bastards. I'm pretty sure I hit one of them."

"Hope the bastard dies! God, my chest is killing me."

"Just be glad you're alive. Still can't believe it. A bulletproof vest! Where'd you get it?"

"A friend gave it to me. I'm never leaving the house again without one, that's for sure."

"Yeah, I gotta buy one now. Just in case, ya know?"

Once they got back to Ronny's place, he said, "Alright, take it off. Let's get a look."

Taking off his shirt was very painful, and lifting his hands in the air just about killed him. After his shirt was off, Ronny helped him remove the vest. Smooth's entire chest was already a big purple bruise.

"Yeah, that might hurt for a few days, but at least you're still alive. Hang on."

Ronny went over to the kitchen, grabbed two glasses, and filled them both with Wild Turkey. Then he stepped into the bathroom, returning a second later.

"Here, take these," Ronny said, handing two pills to Smooth.

"What are these?' Smooth asked.

"Tylenol Threes. They will help with the pain."

"Thanks man. Damn! I can't believe they caught me slipping."

Smooth and Ronny stayed at the kitchen counter drinking until the whole bottle was gone.

"Well, Smooth, I don't think you should be driving, so just crash on the couch, okay?"

"That sounds like a plan."

12

Waking up to loud music, Smooth tried to figure out where he was.

"If she tried to leave, I'm gonna tie her to this bed and set the house on fire," Eminem played loudly in the background.

Smooth's head was pounding and his chest was burning.

So this is what a hangover feels like, he thought.

He remembered getting shot, going back to Ronny's house, and getting drunk.

"Wake up, Sleeping Beauty!" Ronny yelled.

Smooth got up off the couch and walked over to the counter that divided the living room and kitchen. Once there, he sat down on one of the stools. Ronny handed him a glass of orange juice and put a plate of eggs, sausage, and biscuits in front of him. Smooth tore into the food, not realizing how hungry he was. Ronny left for a moment and then returned.

"Here, take these," Ronny said, handing Smooth two more Tylenol Threes.

"Thanks, man!" Smooth responded, going back to eating.

"What are your plans for the day?" Ronny inquired.

"First, I'm going over to a friend's house to thank her for the vest. Then I'm going to catch some lunch at Roxy's. Then probably take care of shopping. I have a few things I need to get."

"Sounds like you got a busy day."

"Yeah. What are your plans?"

"Figure I'd stop in and check on some of our spots, re-stock them, and that's it! Maybe go to a club tonight. Get my party on."

"I'll catch up with you later then," Smooth said, putting the bulletproof vest back on and heading out the door.

Hope these damn pills hurry up and kick in. My damn chest is killing me! Smooth thought.

Getting into his car was very painful. Once inside, he headed to Amanda's. When he arrived, he went to her apartment and knocked. A moment later, the door opened.

"Oh, hey Smooth. I wasn't expecting you for at least a few days. Please, come in," she said, as she opened the door to let him enter.

"Want a drink?"

"Yeah, sure," Smooth answered and followed her into the kitchen.

Her Juicy Couture sweat suit was really showing off her curves.

"So, what brings you by?" she asked.

"I wanted to thank you," he replied.

"Thank me for what?"

"For saving my life!"

"Boy . . . what are you talking about?"

"I was shot yesterday. Four times in the chest!" If it wasn't for that vest, I'd be dead right now."

"Are you kidding me?"

"No, I'm not kidding! Believe me, I wish I were kidding. My chest is killing me."

"Here, take off your shirt and the vest," she instructed, as she helped him remove them.

His chest was one big bruise.

"Here, come into the room," she said, guiding him into her bedroom.

Once there, she had him lay on his back. She grabbed a jar of something and then got on the bed and straddled him. After opening the jar, she stuck in her hand and rubbed the salve all over his chest. After doing it a few times, she started to massage his chest.

"God, that feels good. What is it?"

"It's Icy Hot. It will help some."

After massaging him for 15 minutes, she went and washed her hands and came back into the bedroom. She unbuttoned his pants, unzipped his fly, and reached into his boxers. She then pulled out his dick. She bent over him, putting his dick in her mouth. She sucked him off until he came in her mouth. When she was done, she put his dick back in his pants and then zipped and buttoned his pants again.

"Feel better now?" she asked.

"Yeah, I feel a lot better. Thanks."

"Come on! Let's go back to the kitchen. I need a drink."

"Me too," Smooth agreed, getting up and following her.

"Please make sure you keep the vest on."

"Don't worry. I'll have it on every time I leave the house."

"Good," she replied, pouring him a drink of rum.

After pouring herself a drink as well, she sat down at the table with him.

"So, when you gonna need me again?"

"In probably two or maybe three days. I'm gonna have you do up four this time, if you can."

"I can, but it will take me two days."

"That's okay. No rush. Matter of fact, I got to leave town on Friday, so I'll drop it off then, and I'll pick it up on Sunday when I get back into town."

"Sounds like a plan," she said.

"Well, I don't want to be rude, but I got some shopping to do. So, I gotta go."

"That's cool. I'll see ya on Friday."

"Okay, see ya Friday."

****

At the mall, Smooth headed straight to the Nike Store. After getting two new pairs of Nikes and two new Nike shirts, he headed over to Hop Topic. Inside, he picked up two Affliction shirts and a black light for his room. His next stop was Spencer's, where he bought a dildo and lotion for Miranda as a joke. He then decided to get the same for Roxy. At the cash register, the clerk gave him a weird look.

"The dildos are for my boyfriend," Smooth joked.

The cashier blushed and said, "That's $75.14."

Paying for his purchases, Smooth decided to call it a day and headed for his car. He thought it was time for lunch, so he headed to Roxy's. When he arrived, he grabbed one of the dildos and a bottle of lotion, put them in the bag, and went inside.

The waitress was new, so he said, "My name's Smooth. I have a reserved seat."

144

"Of course, right this way," she led him to his table.

"What can I get you to drink?"

"Coke, no ice, please. Let Roxy know that I am here."

"Sure thing!"

"Returning with his drink, she said, "Roxy said to give her five minutes. Are you ready to order?"

"Yeah. Chicken Alfredo, fried potatoes, and dinner rolls."

"Okay."

Roxy popped up and sat across from him.

"What's good, Smooth?"

"Well, I was at the mall and got to thinking. With you working so much, you probably don't have time for boyfriends, so I picked you up a little present," he told her, handing her the bag.

Reaching in, she pulled out one of the boxes, and her face turned bright red.

"A dildo?" she whispered, looking around as she hurriedly put the box back into the bag. "I can't believe you!"

Smooth burst out laughing.

"You're not funny! Wait until I tell China about this!"

"Hey, she'll probably laugh, too," Smooth joked, still laughing.

"You're probably right!"

"Here's your food," the waitress said, as she set down his plate in front of him.

"Wish I had a camera. We could have made millions on *America's Funniest Home Videos* with that expression on your face."

145

"Fuck you!" she laughed. "I'm gonna get back to work. Enjoy your meal, asshole!" she laughed, as she headed back to the kitchen.

****

Parking his car, he grabbed everything he got from the mall and headed upstairs. Opening the door, Zorro came running up. Closing the door behind him, Smooth went into his bedroom to drop off all his stuff. Once he put everything away, he headed back to the living room and grabbed Zorro's leash. Hooking it on, he headed downstairs and outside. The fresh air felt good. After 30 minutes, he took Zorro back upstairs, and then he headed to Miranda's with the dildo and lotion. Once inside her apartment, he handed her the bag.

"Oh, sex toys! Good, I got an idea," she said.

She pulled a kitchen chair into the living room and put it in front of the couch.

"Sit down here," she instructed, pointing to the chair.

Once he sat down, she started taking off all her clothes. When she was naked, she sat on the couch in front of him, almost close enough to touch. She grabbed the dildo and pulled her legs up onto the couch, and spread them wide open so Smooth could get a good look at her pussy. She then took the dildo and slid it into her hot pussy. Sliding it in and out, she moaned and made sexy faces. It was obvious that she was enjoying herself.

Smooth reached out to touch her, but she slapped his hand away, "No touching! Pull your dick out. I want to watch you masturbate."

He undid his pants and pulled out his hard dick. He grabbed ahold of it and started to stroke it.

"Yeah, keep doing that," she said, as she went back to fucking herself with the dildo.

It was turning Smooth on so much that he had to keep stopping to keep from busting a nut. Suddenly, Miranda moaned real loud and gasped as she came, staring at Smooth masturbating. Smooth stood up, and walked over to her. He got between her legs and slid deep inside her. It was so tight and wet that he came after six strokes, cumming all inside her. Then he pulled out and sat down beside her on the couch.

"Fuck it! I'd know it'd be that good, I would have got that dildo months ago."

"Yeah, it was pretty good, huh?"

"Yes it was!"

"So, what are your plans for the night?" she asked.

"I don't have any plans, why?"

"Just wondering."

"What's on your mind, ma?"

"Just thinking how nice it'd be to have you living with me."

"Well, you already know I got China."

"Yeah, I know. That's the only bad thing. Once China comes home, I'm gonna lose you."

"We will still be friends."

"But I don't want to be just friends. I want us to be more."

"I know you do, but we can't. I'm sorry."

"At least I will have you 'til China comes home. I'll make the best out of it."

"You know, China threw a monkey wrench at me."

"What do you mean?"

"She told me that she and her roommate were lovers, so it'd be okay for me to sleep around."

"Really?"

"Yep. Caught me off guard. She told me how much she loves me and how we're gonna have threesomes when she gets out, and she acts like it's no big deal."

"So, does she know you're sleeping around?"

"I have not told her shit, but the subject has never come up."

"Are you gonna tell her about us?"

"If the subject comes up, yes. But I'm not just going to bring it up like, 'Hey, by the way, I'm sleeping with Miranda again.'"

"Come on, I think we both need a drink," Miranda said, as she put her clothes back on and headed to the kitchen.

Smooth sat down at the kitchen table while Miranda grabbed two glasses and poured them a drink. She then joined him at the table.

"Maybe this should be our last time having sex," she suggested.

"Why?"

"Because I already have feelings for you. And every time we make love, I fall further and further in love, even though I know I'm gonna be heartbroken when China comes home. So maybe it's best we stop now."

"I can understand that; and if that's what you want, I'll respect that."

"Yes, that's what I want. Still friends; just no more sex, okay?"

"Okay."

"Now that that's out of the way, seven of your 10 apartments are rented. I should have you a check tomorrow. I got some people coming tomorrow to check out the other three apartments. I figure I'll have all 10 rented by Monday. How's it feel to be the legal owner of two different apartment building?'

"Feels good. Kinda like I accomplished something."

"You should. Not everyone has a chance to own an apartment building. You should really think about going completely legal. Then you wouldn't have to worry about being shot at."

"Yeah, I know. And I want to go legal, but I can't . . . not right now."

"You should do it while you have a chance. Before you end up dead or in prison."

"I know, I know. Believe me, I know."

"I'm not gonna sit here and beat a dead horse. Just get out while you can."

"I will."

"You know, now that me and you are just friends, I think I'm gonna try Tinder or Match.com. Try to find me a boyfriend."

"Be careful. There's a lot of crazy people out there."

"My luck, I'll hook up with a serial killer. Someone like Ted Bundy or Hannibal Lecter."

"Like I said, a lot of crazy people. Before you date them, check up on them on Facebook and shit to make sure they're not already married. A lot of married guys get on there looking to get a quick piece of ass."

"Don't worry. I'll check on Facebook."

"Good. It's time for me to get ghost. I'll holla at ya tomorrow."

"Alright. See ya tomorrow."

****

Pulling up to Amanda's apartment complex, Smooth looked around. Nothing caught his attention, so he popped open the trunk, got the four kilos out, and headed up to her front door. She answered after the third knock, opening the door in nothing but a bath towel, looking sexy as fuck.

"Damn, girl, you trying to give a nigga a hard-on answering the door with that?' Smooth joked.

"I could have answered it like this," she replied, letting the towel fall to the floor. She stood there butt-ass naked and looking so sexy.

"So, you gonna let me in?"

"Yeah, come on in."

Amanda turned and walked to the kitchen. Smooth stared at her fat ass giggling the whole way. Talk about a sexy walk. Once in the kitchen, Smooth set the bag on the table and then grabbed Amanda, kissing her while grabbing her ass.

"Drop your pants," she ordered.

After taking his pants off, he started to take off his shirt.

"Just sit down," she said.

Once he was in the chair, she straddled him and lowered herself onto his hard cock.

"God, you feel so good inside me."

She picked up the pace, sliding up and down. Smooth watched her breasts bounce up and down on his hard cock.

"Mmmm . . . damn, you feel so good," she moaned.

"Your pussy feels so good, baby."

"Oh, God! I'm fixing to cum," she said.

"Me, too!" Smooth agreed, as he tensed up and busted his nut inside her.

"Here I cummmm! Oh God! I'm cumming!" she screamed, riding him faster.

After she came, they just sat there, locked in place until she finally stood up.

"I love the way you feel when you cum inside of me," she added.

Out of all the girls he slept with, Amanda had the best pussy— better than everyone except China did. China's pussy was number one. Walking over to the counter, Amanda poured them both a drink and handed a glass to Smooth.

"Let me go put some clothes on."

"Alright."

Smooth slapped her on the ass as she walked by. A few minutes later, she returned wearing some Lucky jeans and a tight miniskirt that hugged her body and showed off her flat stomach.

"You are so sexy. You know that?" he asked.

"Yeah, right! You probably say that to all the women!" she joked.

"Nah, I'm serious."

"This the four keys?" she asked, changing the subject and grabbing the bag.

"Yeah, that's the four keys. I'll be back to get them on Sunday."

"I'll have them all done and bagged by then."

"Thanks."

"So, where you going?"

"To visit my girl. She's in prison."

"So you got a girl, huh?"

"Yeah, but it's a weird relationship. She knows what I do."

"And she's okay with it?"

"It was actually her idea. She didn't want me to catch a bad case of the blue balls."

"Very funny."

"I'm actually being serious. She is sleeping with her roommate."

"Sleeping with her roommate?"

"Yeah! Like I said, it's a weird relationship."

"How long 'til she gets out?"

"About two and a half years."

"Guess I better enjoy you while I can then."

"Yeah, guess so."

"Well, these will be done when you get back."

"Okay, I'm gonna go ahead and get on the road."

"Drive safe."

"I will."

Smooth gave her a kiss and then headed to his car. As soon as he got in his car, the phone rang.

"Hello."

"Hey man, just checking on ya. Wanna go out tonight?" Ronny asked.

"Nah, I'm on my way out of town to visit China."

"Alright, see ya when you get back."

****

After grabbing them some food, Smooth sat down at the table to wait for China. Five minutes later, she entered the visiting area. As soon as she saw him, she broke into a big smile. He stood up and hugged her, giving her a long kiss. Then they both sat down.

"I got us both pizzas and chicken sandwiches, since I know you like them."

"Yeah, it tastes good."

She removed the bottom bun of the chicken sandwich, and then set the top bun and chicken on the pizza. She then picked it up and took a big bite.

"Yummmm! This is so good," she said.

Smooth did what did she did and then took a big bite. He was surprised how good it tasted. Smooth opened a bag of Doritos and set them in the middle of the table so they could share them.

"So, how's everything at home?"

"Good, other than missing you. Zorro has gotten so big."

"Tell him mommy misses him."

"When I get home, I'll take some pictures for ya and sent them."

"That'd be really nice. I have a few pictures of us together that Roxy sent me, but I'd like some more."

"I got ya."

"Roxy told me about the dildo," China laughed.

"I told her you'd laugh."

"Wish I could have been there."

"You should have seen her face. It was priceless!"

"I bet. She's always been easy to embarrass."

"Yeah. So how you holding up in here?"

"I'm good. It's rough missing you all, but I'm holding in there."

"That's my girl!"

"Remember, Rebecca gets out on Wednesday, so you got to be here before 9:00 a.m."

"I'll be here. I think I'm gonna go to New York and re-up while I'm already out of town. So let her know we won't be going straight home."

"I'll let her know. Smooth, I gotta ask you something."

"Just ask, baby."

"We always talked about our future. About badass cars we'd have, big houses, traveling the world and shit. But we never talked about kids or marriage. Why?"

"I don't know. Guess we never got around to it."

Damn, Smooth thought, *first Amanda talking about kids and marriage and now China.* But then again, it was a big difference, because he could see himself setting down with China because he loved her.

"Well, would you marry me?" she asked.

"Yeah, I would. How about we set a date for when you get out?"

"And what about kids? Would you want kids?

"I'd love for you to have my kids. I'd want at least two kids—a boy and a girl. How about you?"

"Two sounds good. But we'd have to find a house. That way, we would have a backyard for the kids to play in. Where we live now is nice, but not for kids. We'd definitely have to move to a house with a yard."

"How about I start looking for houses now? I already bought two apartment buildings. So might as well buy a house and have it ready for when you get out."

They finished up their visit by coming up with baby names. And Smooth promised to be there to pick up Rebecca.

****

Smooth called Banga when he got close to Stuart.

"Yellow?"

"Hey, yo! What's ya up to?"

"Oh, hey Smooth. I was just fixing to call you."

"Why, what's up?"

"I need a few more of those things."

"Well, you're in luck, my friend. I'm in Stuart, and I have three of them with me."

"Good. Meet me at the apartment."

"Alright."

A few minutes later, Smooth pulled up to the apartment and saw Banga, Meka, and Ham all sitting outside.

"What's up, B?" Ham asked, giving Smooth dap.

Meka stood up and gave him a big hug and kiss.

"Good to see ya again, daddy. Are you gonna have time for me?"

"Hell ya, baby!"

"You got those three?"

"Yeah, come on," Smooth said, leading Banga around to the trunk. Popping open the trunk, Smooth reached in, grabbed the bag, and handed it to Banga.

"Come on. I'll get your money," he replied, leading Smooth and the others into the apartment.

Banga went over to the table, dumped out the kilos, and then started stuffing money into the bag. Once he was finished, he zipped up the bag and handed it back to Smooth.

"Hey Meka!"

"Yeah?"

"Let me put this in the car, and then I'll be right back.'

"Okay, daddy."

Smooth ran the money out to the car and returned.

"Come on daddy," Meka said, grabbing Smooth's hand and leading him to the back bedroom.

Once they were in and the doors closed, Meka started taking off her clothes.

"Come on, get undressed!"

When they were both naked, she pushed him onto the bed and climbed on top. Sliding down on his hard cock, she gasped and sat still for a minute, biting her bottom lip. Then she started riding his cock up and down until they both started to cum at the same time.

"Thank you, daddy, for letting me please you. Mmmmm!"

She slid down and took his soft cock into her mouth. Within minutes, she had him hard again. The way she was deep throating him, and humming while she sucked him dick, was driving him crazy, until he emptied his load in her mouth. She kept sucking until he was bone dry.

"Shit, you taste good, daddy," she said, getting up and getting dressed. Following her lead, Smooth then got up and got dressed

"Well, I'm sorry, but I got to go," he told her.

"That's okay."

He kissed her and headed to his car. Outside, he saw Banga so he stopped to give him dap.

"I'm outta here, dawg."

"Alright, catch ya next time."

****

On the way home, Smooth started thinking of his last talk with Miranda. The stuff she said was real. He had enough money to get out of the game and go legal, but he couldn't. He couldn't explain it. The streets called to him. He grew up on the streets. The streets were all he really knew. The streets were his house.

As he continued thinking about this, his phone rang. Looking at the display, he didn't recognize the number.

"Hello?"

"Hey Smooth?"

"Who is this?" Smooth asked.

"It's me, Missy."

"Oh, hey baby girl. What's good?"

"Just thinking about you, wanting to know if you'd want to hang out."

"Sure. Where you at?"

"My apartment."

"Alright. Give me 30 minutes, and I'll be there."

"Okay, see you then."

Smooth reached his apartment building as he was hanging up. He rushed upstairs, opened the door, and as soon as he entered, he was almost knocked off his feet by Zorro.

"Hey there, big guy. Ready for a walk?" he asked, grabbing Zorro's leash.

After he walked Zorro, he took a quick shower and then put on a Polo Ralph Lauren outfit with some Bottega Veneta boots and headed out the door. Five minutes later, he was at Missy's door. Before he could knock, the door opened.

"You said 30 minutes. It's been 45 minutes!"

"Sorry."

"No problem. I'm just busting you balls."

"So what are we gonna do?"

"Figured we'd lay around my place and watch some movies."

"Sounds good."

"I got chips, dip, and rum with Mountain Dew."

"Yum . . . perfect."

Sitting on the couch and eating, they started to watch *White House Down* with Jamie Foxx and Channing Tatum.

"Don't know about you, but I'm starving, and these chips ain't working," Smooth said.

"Well, let's order a pizza."

"Meat lover's deep dish."

"Sounds good. I'll go order it," she said, going to the kitchen. He paused the movie so she wouldn't miss anything. She returned in a few minutes and sat back down on the couch.

"They said it would be about 30 minutes."

"Thought it was 30 minutes or less . . . or it's free"

"That's Domino's. I ordered Pizza Hut."

"Shit, Pizza Hut has the best pizza."

"Back to the movie!" she said, grabbing the remote from him and pushing play.

"Do you think this could really happen?"

"What?"

"Terrorists taking over the White House?"

"I don't know. That place is built like Fort Knox, but armed better. Those Secret Service people don't play around."

Knock, knock, knock.

"That must be the pizza. I'll get it," Smooth said, getting up and going to the door. Sure enough, it was the pizza. Smooth gave the guy a $20 and told him to keep the change. Walking back to the couch, Smooth set the pizza on the coffee table, opened the box, pulled out a piece, and took a big bite.

"Now this is what I'm talking about!" he said.

"Mmmmmm . . . this is good!"

"Yes, it is!"

They sat there and ate the pizza while they finished watching the movie. When the movie was over, Missy said, "Now it's time for my favorite movie: *Pretty Woman.*"

"That's your favorite movie?"

"Yeah, why?"

"Just asking. Let's watch it."

Smooth was actually enjoying the movie. About 35 minutes into the movie, a sex scene made Smooth's dick get hard. He adjusted himself, trying to make room for his hard-on. Missy noticed and leaned over and undid his pants. Pulling them down, she pulled out his hard cock and put it in her mouth.

"Mmmm," she mumbled, when she placed it into her wet mouth. She began to suck it.

"Damn!" Smooth answered, as he grabbed Missy's hair and started fucking her mouth like a pussy.

"Mmmmm . . . mmmm," Missy moaned, as the juices ran down her mouth and neck.

Smooth continued to fuck her mouth until he came inside her mouth. She continued sucking until she swallowed all his cum.

"Get up and get undressed" Smooth ordered Missy.

After she undressed, Smooth, told her to bend over the couch. She did as she was told. Smooth grabbed her around the waist and slid all the way into her tight pussy, causing her to gasp. He pulled out and then slid back in hard and fast.

"Yessss . . . give it to me, baby," she moaned.

With every moan, he fucked her harder. Her moans and gasps really turned him on. He continued to pound her pussy until she came. Once she came, Smooth laid her on the floor, put her legs on his shoulders, and slid off in her. He continued to fuck her until he busted a nut in her. Afterwards, he lay down beside her on the floor trying to catch his breath.

"I think we missed the movie," Missy joked.

"That's alright; I had my own pretty woman to entertain me."

"Very entertaining."

"Glad to hear that. You weren't bad yourself."

"Are you kidding me? I'm the best!"

"Yeah, you are."

"Thanks. Now do we rewind the movie, or do we just start another one?"

"Let's start another one."

They spent the rest of the night watching movies until Smooth and Missy began to doze off.

"Let's go to bed," Missy suggested.

Smooth fell asleep as soon as his head hit the pillow.

13

After knocking on Amanda's door, he waited for her to answer. When she did, she stood on her tippy toes to give him a kiss.

"You had me so worried."

"I know I said I'd be here Sunday, but something came up and I couldn't make it."

"I waited all day and all night. You could have at least called me."

"I know. I'm sorry."

"I forgive you, but don't let it happen again, okay?"

"Okay."

"Now, come on in," she said, as she led him into the kitchen and poured him a drink. After taking a sip, it burned all the way down.

"What the hell is this?"

"It's Jack Daniels. I'm out of rum."

"Next time warn me."

"Don't be a baby. Just drink it," she replied playfully. She was looking sexy as always, wearing tight low-riding jeans, a tight belly shirt, and sandals.

"Shit, ma, you looking good in that outfit. You plan on going out or something?"

"Nah, just gonna go get my nails done and do some shopping."

"You need a ride?"

"Nope. Got my girlfriend is coming over. We do it once or twice a week."

"Just make sure you all are careful. It's a crazy world out there."

"I know."

"Here's your money," he said, handing her an envelope.

"Your stuff's all in the bag."

"Alright. I guess I'm gonna get ghost before your friend shows. I'll see you in a few days."

"I'll be looking forward to it."

Smooth gave her a kiss and then headed out to his car. He opened the trunk with the remote, threw the bag in, and closed it. Getting behind the wheel, he put on a Big Sean CD, cranked it up, and then headed to Ronny's.

****

Smooth saw Guru's blacked-out Dodge Charger sitting behind Ronny's Lexus. Smooth looked around. Not seeing anything out of place, he got out and walked up to Ronny's door. He could hear Flo-Rida bumping inside. Smooth banged on the door loud, so Ronny could hear over the music.

Ronny opened the door and screamed, "Damn, why you trying to knock a nigga's door down?"

"Just wanted you to hear me over the music."

"We heard you. Damn, thought the police were at my door the way you were banging!"

"Can I come in or we gonna stand here all day?"

"Come on in."

When Smooth got inside, he saw Guru playing Xbox while sitting on the couch.

"So what's good, my nigga?" Ronny asked.

"Nothing. Just thought I'd pop up and see what's happening."

"Business is doing good. No problems lately."

"Well, I'm gonna be going out of town on Tuesday, and won't be back until probably Thursday."

"Alright, we should be good 'til then with two more."

"Shit, I forgot! Be right back," Smooth said and he ran out to his car, looked around, popped the trunk, pulled out the bag with the four cooked keys, and came back inside.

"This here is four keys. Double what I been giving you, so it should last until I get back."

"Yeah, that should definitely do."

"If there is any problem, call me."

"I will. But I really don't see anything going wrong."

"Never know. Anything new with the damn Mexicans?"

"No, not since they shot you."

"All right, I'm out of here. See you on Thursday or Friday."

****

Sitting on the bench watching a movie, China told Rebecca, "I'll be back. Gotta use the bathroom."

"Okay. I'll hold your spot."

China entered her cell and hung up a sheet for privacy so that it would look as if she was using the bathroom. She opened up her locker, pulled out a honey bun, a peanut butter squeeze, and a bag of peanut M&Ms. Opening the honey bun, she set it on top of the plastic and then set it on the locker. She then opened the peanut butter squeeze and spread it over the bun. She then crushed up the M&Ms and sprinkled them all over the top, making a nice homemade cake. Then she split the cake into two pieces using her inmate ID card. Taking down the sheet, she grabbed both pieces of cake, went back and sat down beside Rebecca, and handed her one piece of the cake.

"A little going-away present," China said, taking a bite of her cake.

Rebecca took a bite of the cake and moaned, "This is good. Thanks!"

"I know it's not much, but it's the best I could do here."

"You didn't have to do anything."

"I know, but I did."

"Alright, ladies, its lockdown time, so head to your cells," screamed the guard over the intercom.

China and Rebecca both got up and headed to their cell while finishing their cake. Once inside the cell, the door locked.

"I am gonna miss you, but I'm sure in the hell not going to miss this place!"

"I feel ya."

"I'm not gonna know how to act without having to hear those dumb-ass guards all the time."

"Well, tomorrow's the big day. What's the first thing you're gonna want to do?"

"Shit! Get some real food."

"Mmmmm . . . real food sounds good. What next?"

"Find some good dick!" she laughed.

"Bitch, you gonna have Smooth right there. That's all the good dick you gonna need."

"China, I'm just not sure I'm comfortable sleeping with your man."

"Hell, Rebecca, I'm giving you permission; and believe me, once you see him in person, you'll want to."

"I've never been with a black guy before. Heck, I've only been with two guys."

"Trust me, Smooth will take good care of you, and he will teach you a thing or two. I know you both are gonna like each other. The two loves of my life together. You can pleasure each other until I get home. Then it will be the three of us."

"Sounds almost too good to be true."

"It's true!"

"What if he don't like me?"

"Don't worry, he will. I know what he likes and doesn't like."

China moved next to Rebecca and started kissing her and sliding her hands over her ass.

"Take off your clothes," China ordered.

Without a word, Rebecca got naked. China stepped out of her clothes and lay down on the bed on her back.

"Sit on my face. I want to 69!"

Rebecca straddled China's face. She then leaned down, spread her pussy lips with her fingers, and stated licking as if she was licking icing off a cake. China moaned out loudly while she started to suck, lick, and nibble on Rebecca's clit, while sliding two fingers in and out of her tight pussy. Rebecca's pussy was so tight that she could barely get two fingers inside it. She didn't know how Smooth was going to fit his big dick inside her. Just thinking about it turned China on even more, however.

"Agggh . . . I'm gonna cummmm . . ." Rebecca gasped, as she exploded all over China's face.

Rebecca sat still for a minute and then went back to licking and sucking China's pussy. Thinking of Smooth and Rebecca set China off in a big orgasm. Rebecca continued to lick China's pussy until she got every last drop.

****

Sitting on the hood of his car outside of Lowell Correctional Institution, waiting on Rebecca to get out, Smooth couldn't believe he was doing this: sitting outside a prison waiting to pick up some bitch he didn't even know. Hell, he didn't even know what she looked like. What if she looked like some bull dyke? China couldn't expect him to sleep with that. But he was doing this for China because he loved her.

He heard the gate open and looked in that direction. He couldn't believe his eyes. Out walked the most beautiful woman he had ever seen with long red hair and a body like Kim Kardashian. She had big tits, a slim waist, and a fat ass. Her walk was totally sexy, with her swaying hips and bouncing tits and ass.

She called, "Smooth?"

"Yeah, that's me."

She got to the car and started to jump up and down yelling, "I'm free!"

She threw her arms around Smooth and stood on her tippy toes to kiss him. Not a big kiss, just a little peck on the lips. But it still caught Smooth off guard. Smooth hugged her and gave her a peck on the lips. She pulled away from him.

"Sorry. You must think I'm crazy."

"Not really. Well maybe a little," he joked.

"I'm just so excited to be free after five years."

"I can understand that."

"Good, can we get the hell away from here, before they decide to take me back?"

"Come on," Smooth said, opening the passenger door for her. After he closed her door and got into the car himself. He handed her the CDs and told her to pick one. She chose a Chris Brown CD.

"Any particular place you wanna go before we get on our way?"

"Burger King."

"Alright, next stop is Burger King."

"I really appreciate you picking me up."

"No problem."

"So, China said we are going up north to do something before we go back to Miami, right?"

"Yeah, gotta go to New York to handle some business."

"Well, I'm down for whatever. I'm just glad to be out of that place!"

Pulling up next to Burger King, Smooth decided to go inside instead of the drive-thru. Once inside, everyone's heads turned when they saw Rebecca in a tight skirt and blouse. Smooth couldn't blame them. Once they got to the counter to order, the poor, young brother couldn't stop staring at her.

A bit tongue-tied, he finally snapped out of it and managed to say, "Welcome to Burger King. How can I help you?"

"I'll take a Whopper, large fries, large order of chicken tenders, and a Mountain Dew," she replied.

"I'll have the same as her."

After paying for their food and getting it, they sat down in a booth towards the back. All the men kept looking at her. Hell, he couldn't take his eyes off her either.

"You got everyone's attention, ma. They can't stop staring."

"I'm used to it. The only attention I need is yours."

"Well, you got it."

"So, if you don't mind me asking, what was you in prison for?"

"China didn't tell you?"

"Nah."

"I killed my boyfriend for looking at another girl."

"Whaaa . . ." Smooth about choked on his food.

She busted out laughing, "I'm just joking. I got caught passing bad checks."

"I heard of people doing that. Was it good money?"

"Yeah, it was. But I learned that fake credit cards make a lot more."

"What do you mean fake credit cards?"

"You get a credit card in someone else's name and buy everything with it."

"Sounds simple."

"Really, it is. The trick is to not hit the same place too many times. You gotta move around."

"So what are you gonna do for money now?"

"Not really sure to tell you the truth."

"Well, are you wanting to go legit or what?"

"Not really sure. Gotta give it some thought."

"Well, let me know when you decide. I might be able to help in some way."

"Like how?"

"Not sure. But I know lots of people and have lots of contacts."

"I'll let you know soon as I figure it out."

****

"Wake up, Sleeping Beauty," Smooth said.

"Ohhhh, sorry. I must have dozed off. Are we there?"

"No. Just stopping to get gas and something to eat."

"Okay," Rebecca replied, getting out of the car and stretching.

Damn! Smooth thought, *she got a killer body.*

"They got a Subway inside. Are you okay with that?" he asked.

"Subway sounds good."

They both headed inside. Once they got up to the counter, Smooth saw that the normal $5 foot-longs were now $6.

"What's up with the $6 foot-longs?" he asked.

"They raised them up last weekend," the cashier replied.

"Why?"

"Don't know, I'm just the cashier. They don't tell us shit!"

"I feel ya on that. Give me a foot-long Italian sub."

"I want the same," Rebecca agreed.

Once they got their sandwiches, they went to the gas station and Smooth paid for gas and headed to the car.

"Go ahead and get in while I pump the gas.

"Alright."

Smooth watched her get into the car. He leaned down and looked at her through the driver's side window. When she got in, her short skirt rode up her thighs, giving him a good shot of her white G-string. She adjusted her skirt and then opened her sandwich. When he was done pumping the gas, he got into the car and pulled into a parking spot so they could eat.

"Never had one of these before. They are good."

"It's my favorite sub."

"I've only eaten here one time and I had the turkey club."

"Never ate that. My next favorite is chicken strips with bacon."

"Now that sounds good."

"It is! Probably a lot better than what you been eating for the last five years," he joked.

"Hell, anything's better than that shit."

"Damn, I'm tired."

"How much further we got?"

"About four hours."

"Want me to drive so you can rest up some?"

"Sure, that'd be nice."

"They got out and switched places. Rebecca's got to move the seat all the way up to reach the pedals.

"Okay, now how do you put in go mode?"

"What?"

"How do you make it go? Just push a pedal or do I got to do something else?"

"You never drove before?'

"Yes, I'm just giving you a hard time," she said, as she put it in gear, backed out, and then headed to the highway.

"You had me there for a minute," he laughed.

"You got a nice laugh. You should do it more."

"Well, you got a sexy smile, and really should smile more."

"Well, I really haven't had much to smile about in these last five years, but I've smiled a lot since I met China."

"Yeah, China could make anyone smile."

"She is a really good person."

"To her friends, yeah. But you don't want to get on her bad side. She can be one mean bitch!" Smooth laughed.

"I bet. I know I'm really lucky to have met her. Meeting her is one of the best things that's ever happened to me."

"You sound like you really love her!"

"I do. I love her more than I can put into words. I know she loves me back, and I also know how much she loves you. All she could talk about was you and us three together."

"Every time she called or we had a visit, she'd talk about you. So I know she loves you, too. I'm just not sure what she expects from us. Like, is she expecting us to become lovers?"

"Yes. She wants us to become lovers and keep each other happy until she gets out and can be with both of us. She wants the three of us to all be together."

"I want what she wants. If she's happy, I'm happy. What about you?"

"To be honest, I'm not sure what I want. But I'm willing to give it a try for China."

"What . . . you don't find me sexy enough?" she laughed.

"Oh, believe me . . . you're sexy enough! You're one of the most beautiful women I've ever met."

"Why thank you."

"Wake me up when we get to New York, okay?"

"Okay."

14

"Wake up! We're here!" Rebecca said, pulling Smooth out of a fitful sleep.

"What time is it?" Smooth asked, rubbing his eyes.

"It's 10:23 a.m. We just got into New York. Where do we go now?"

"Let's find the mall."

"Okay, let's stop for directions."

After pulling into a gas station, Rebecca got out and went inside to ask for directions. Smooth was watching her every step of the way. Her hips were swaying and her ass was jiggling. When she came back out, he watched her hips sway and her tits bounce. Smooth had never seen a more beautiful woman. Nor had he ever seen such a hypnotic walk that screamed, "Look at me!" Once back in the car, Rebecca put the car into drive and pulled off.

"Good news. We are not far."

"Can't wait to get out and stretch some."

"What are we going to the mall for?"

"You'll see."

"I hate surprises. No, I don't. I just don't like not knowing."

"Well, you'll know soon enough."

After a few wrong turns, they finally found the mall and got a parking spot. Inside, Smooth started looking for a cell phone store.

Finding one, he told Rebecca, "Pick one out."

"Ummmm . . . the pink one."

"Alright. I want the pink IPhone 6 plus with the unlimited package. And I want a Miami number."

"Anything else, sir?"

"Nope."

Getting that all taken care of, Smooth walked to the food court.

"Look, I got to go handle some business. It will only take me about an hour. Here . . ." Smooth said, as he handed Rebecca a knot of bills. "There's $5,000. I want you to buy some clothes and anything else you might need. I will call you when I'm done, and we will meet right back here in the food court."

"I'll be waiting for you to call me."

"Like I said, it will be about an hour. Do all the shopping you can."

****

Pulling up to the gate, Smooth waited for the guard. A few moments later, the guard walked over to Smooth.

"Ah, yes, I remember you. Smooth, right?"

"Yes, that's me!"

How the hell did he remember me, Smooth wondered.

A minute later, the guard came back, opened the gate, and waved Smooth through.

Smooth followed the long, curvy driveway all the way up to the house where he was met by two other guards. Smooth got out of the car and walked to the trunk, opened it with the keyless remote, grabbed the money, and closed the trunk.

Walking up to the door, one of the guards said, "Follow me, please."

Smooth was led into the same library as the last few times. Setting the money on a couch, Smooth looked around and noticed three walls covered with books. Most of them looked to be leather-bound. The fourth wall was one large window with a great view of a lake or pond. It was huge though.

Hearing someone enter the room, Smooth expected it to be the guard to lead him to the pool as usual, so he went to grab the money. But before he could grab the bag, he got a good a good look at the person and was surprised.

"Jefe?"

"Hello, my friend. How are things going?"

"Thangs goin' good."

Another person entered the room. It was Raul. Jefe said something to him in Spanish and then pointed to the money and said something else. Smooth picked up the bag and handed it to Raul. After Raul was gone, a beautiful Spanish lady walked in and asked Jefe something.

Jefe then asked Smooth, "Would you like something to drink?"

"Sure. Rum and Coke would be nice."

As soon as gave his order, the lady turned around and left, returning a few minutes later with two drinks. Jefe waited until she left before he spoke.

"I hear you're having a little problem down south with some Mexicans."

"Yeah, but it will be taken care of soon."

"I hope so. I hate wars, especially ones that involved my customers."

"Don't worry. It will be taken care of."

"Let me know if I can be of assistance."

"Not to change the subject, but it looks like someone likes to read."

"It's funny. I never imagined I'd be a bookworm, but in prison, I found a love for reading. I'd rather read than watch television. The books are always more interesting to me. What about you?"

"I read *To Kill a Mockingbird* in school, and I hated it!"

"That's probably just the book itself. The trick is to find a good book. Once you find a good book, you'll never want to put it down until the end."

"I might give it a try."

"Being black and living the life you live, you might want to check out a few urban novels."

"Where do I get them?"

"Ummm . . . Jefe walked over to a book shelf. He looked a minute, pulled out a book from the shelf, and handed it to Smooth.

"*Never Be the Same,* by Silk White," Smooth read the cover.

"It's a good book. Very interesting. Give it a try. I believe you will like it if you give it a try."

"I'll read it, and I'll let you know what I think about it."

Raul returned and said something in Spanish to Jefe. He then handed a bag to Smooth and left the room.

"Well, my friend, drive safe. Don't forget to call and let me know you've made it back safe."

"I'll call as soon as I get home."

****

Arriving back at the mall, Smooth parked as close as he could to the Macy's. He then got out and headed inside. Once he entered the mall, he pulled out his smart phone and called Rebecca.

"Hey handsome. Calling for a good time?" she answered.

"You done shopping?"

"Yes, I'm at the food court now."

"I'm on my way," Smooth replied, before hanging up.

Once he arrived at the food court, it was easy to spot Rebecca. Her bright red hair really stood out. He walked over to her table and saw that she had a shitload of bags.

"Ready to go? Or do you need more time?"

"I'm ready to go. I'm all shopped out."

Smooth grabbed some of the bags and led the way back to the car. Popping open the trunk, Smooth put all the bags inside and then closed it and got inside the car.

"Are you hungry?" Smooth asked.

"I'm starving."

"How about Long John Silvers?"

"Sounds great!"

Instead of going through the drive-thru, they went inside. After getting their food and sitting down, Smooth messed with her.

"I can't believe you ordered chicken at a seafood place."

"Hey, it's the best chicken in the world. It's in the batter. Plus, I hate fish!"

"The best chicken, huh?"

"Here, try it," she offered, giving him a piece.

"Yummm . . . you're right, it's definitely good. I didn't even know they sold chicken here."

"Well, now you know."

Smooth's phone rang.

"Hello?"

"Yes, is dis Smooth?"

"Yes, it's me, Stone."

"Tis good to speak to you."

"Well, what can I do for you?"

"Yes, remember dat last talk?"

"Yes, I remember, Stone."

"Good, 'cause I need six of doz tings."

"Meet me . . . better yet . . . call me this time tomorrow, and we will set up a time to meet, okay?"

"Okay, mon. I'll call tomorrow."

After hanging up, Smooth finished his meal. Rebecca finished before him and then started to take French fries off his plate.

"You always eat like this?"

"Yep. I got a high metabolism. Never gain a pound."

"I don't think I've ever met a woman who didn't worry about gaining weight."

"I like my body. I don't need to lose or gain a single pound."

"You're right about that. You have an excellent body."

"Well, thank you."

"You're welcome."

"Do you ever worry about gaining or losing weight?"

"Nah, never even gave it a thought. But I'm only 17, so I think I'm good."

"You're only 17?"

"Yeah. Why, how old are you?"

"Take a guess!"

"21?"

"Nope, 26."

"And you still fly?"

"Well, you ready to get back on the road? We got a long trip."

"Ready when you are."

Walking out to the car, Smooth opened the door for Rebecca.

"Aww! The perfect gentleman."

"Yeah, that's me!"

****

After pulling into the garage, Smooth got out and looked around while Rebecca was getting out of the car. Looking around, Smooth didn't detect anything out of the ordinary, so he popped the trunk. Rebecca walked back to the trunk and helped Smooth grab all the bags. After closing the trunk, Smooth led the way to the elevator. Once they stepped out, Smooth set the bags down and opened the door. Inside, Smooth headed to the spare bedroom.

"This is your bedroom," Smooth said, stepping inside and laying the bags on the bed.

"Thanks."

"The bathroom is right here," Smooth said, pointing across the hall.

"Well, I guess I will put everything away and then take a nice long bath."

"I gotta go get Zorro and then I'll be back."

"Zorro?"

"Yeah, China's pit bull."

"Okay."

"Don't open the door for anyone. I have a key."

"Okay."

Smooth took off out the door. Once in front of Miranda's door, Smooth knocked three times.

Boom, boom, boom.

Almost immediately, the door flung open and Zorro growled until he saw Smooth.

"Once he saw him, he let out a whine and a playful bark . . . his tail wagging a hundred miles an hour. Miranda grabbed Zorro to keep him from running out the door, and then she stepped back for him to enter.

Once Smooth was inside, she asked, "Care for a drink?"

"Yes and please make it strong. I'm really going to need it."

"Why, what's wrong?"

"Well, you know how I told you China was sleeping with her roommate?"

"Yeah?"

"Well, China decided to let her have our spare bedroom without even asking me. So I had to drive up to Ocala, pick her up, and now she's gonna be living with me."

"And you're allowing it?"

"Yeah, but only because it's what China wants."

"Why do I guess there's more to it than that?"

"There is."

"So . . . ?"

"China has it in her head that she wants me and Rebecca to become lovers and to keep each other happy until she gets out, and then all three of us can be together."

"How do you feel about that?"

"Not really sure."

"Is this Rebecca cute?"

"She's more than cute. She's beautiful!"

"So would you have a problem sleeping with her?"

"I guess not."

"Well then, you have every guy's dream of two beautiful women."

"Yeah, but it's just weird. I don't even know this Rebecca, and now she is living with me."

"Well, get to know her then."

"How?"

"Just like you got to know me. Talk to her. Ask her questions. Duh!"

"I guess I'm just overthinking it."

"Sounds like it."

"Well, I better get back downstairs."

"Okay. I'll see ya."

Smooth grabbed Zorro's leash, attached it, and headed to the elevator. In his apartment, he took off Zorro's leash, as the dog took off into the living room barking and tail wagging. When Smooth got to the living room, he saw Rebecca bent down petting Zorro.

"He's so cute."

"Yes, he is," Smooth agreed.

He then took out his smart phone and took a few pictures of Zorro and Rebecca together for China. Rebecca stood up and Smooth saw that she was wearing low-riding Miss Me jeans and a wife-beater. She looked absolutely hot.

"Well, how do I look?" she asked.

"Beautiful, sexy, and, oh yeah, SEXY!"

"So what's for dinner?"

"Figured we'd go to Roxy's. It's a restaurant owned by China's sister."

"Sounds good."

"Everything on the menu is good."

****

At Roxy's, Smooth led Rebecca to his table. A few moments later, a waitress came to the table.

"What can I get you all to drink?"

"Coke, no ice," Smooth answered.

"Mountain Dew," Rebecca said.

"Also, could you let Roxy know I'm here?"

"Sure thing."

"This is a nice place."

"Yeah, and the food is excellent. Normally all the tables are full."

"Hmmmm . . . so what would you recommend to eat?"

"Well, I'm having chicken Alfredo. It's really good."

"That's what I'll take then."

"Here's your drinks," the waitress said, setting them down in front of them.

"You decided what you want to eat?"

"We will both have the chicken Alfredo and fried potatoes."

"Alright."

As soon as the waitress left, Roxy sat down next to Smooth.

"So, Smooth, who's your friend?"

"Oh, Roxy, this is China's roommate, Rebecca. Rebecca, this is China's sister, Roxy."

"Nice to meet you, Rebecca."

"Same here. This is a nice place you have here."

"Why, thank you very much. Well, Smooth, if you all need anything, just ask. But for now, I gotta get back to work."

"Alright," Smooth said.

"So, do you have any brothers or sisters?" Rebecca asked.

"No. What about you?"

"I got a brother. He's in the army somewhere. I haven't seen him or talked to him in at least five years."

"Why not?"

"I lost contact with him when I got locked up because they took my cell phone which had his number in it. So I had no other way to reach him. I don't even think he knows I got locked up."

"Well, I know someone who can track him down for you if you want."

"That'd be really nice. I'd love to talk to him."

"I'll contact him tomorrow then."

"Okay."

"Here's your food," the waitress said, coming up and putting the plates on the table.

"Eat up!"

****

Back at the apartment, Smooth grabbed Zorro's leash.

"Come on, boy!" he called for Zorro.

"Rebecca?"

"Yeah?"

"I'm gonna take Zorro out for a walk. Remember; don't open the door for anyone. I have a key."

"See ya when you get back."

Downstairs while walking Zorro, Smooth's phone rang.

"Hello?"

"You back in town yet?" Ronny asked.

"Just got back. Why, what's up?"

"Gonna need to re-up soon. Running low."

"I will be there tomorrow, alright?"

"Yea, see ya then."

After 20 minutes, Smooth and Zorro headed back upstairs. In the apartment, Zorro went into the living room. Reaching the living room, Smooth was surprised to see Rebecca standing there looking like a Victoria Secret model in a lace bra and G-string.

"Wow!"

"That's all you got to say?"

"Double wow!"

Smooth was getting hard just looking at her. Her breasts looked like they were fixing to pop out. The G-string was barely the size of a postage stamp.

"Come here," she said, taking his hand and leading him to her room.

Following her, Smooth couldn't help but watch her ass. Once inside the room, Rebecca closed the door and told Smooth to undress. After taking off his clothes, he stood there waiting on her. She was staring at his hard cock.

"Oh my God!" she said.

"What?"

"That thing is huge! I don't know if I can handle all that!"

"Why not?"

"I've only been with two guys and both of them were half that size."

"So you want me to put my clothes back on?"

"Hell no! I'm gonna try it."

Smooth walked over to her, grabbed her, and started to kiss her while grabbing her ass. He told her to get undressed. After she stripped naked, Smooth kissed her and led her to the bed. Laying her down, Smooth trailed kisses to her breasts, sucking on one of her nipples while massaging the other one. Then he continued south until he reached her pussy. He was surprised to find it freshly shaved.

"Nice!" he said.

Never having been with a woman who shaved her pussy, he slid one finger inside while licking her. *Damn, she's tight*, he thought. *Real tight.* Smooth started to think that she was right and that he might not fit. He didn't know a pussy could be so tight, but he was damn sure going to try.

"Mmmmmm . . ." she moaned.

She smelled like strawberries and tasted just as sweet. He tried putting two fingers in her while sucking, licking, and nibbling on her clit, which was driving her crazy. Her moans turned him on even more. Without warning, she reached orgasm and exploded all over his face. He stood up, spread her legs, and slid his hard cock into her tight pussy. He barely got two inches in before she moaned all over again. He pushed even deeper inside her. About halfway in, she gasped and told him to stop.

"Let me get adjusted to it."

He pulled out slowly, sliding back in halfway.

After doing this a few times, she said, "Okay, give me more."

He slid in even more and heard her catch her breath. He pulled out and then slid back in really slowly, taking his time. Her pussy was so tight that he wasn't going to last very long. Damn, this is the best pussy he had ever had. Even better than China's. Finally, he got all the way in. He started to fuck her with long strokes. She came again and he picked up speed. She felt him deep in her stomach. Finally, not being able to take it any longer, he exploded deep inside her tight pussy.

"Damn, girl!"

"Oh my God! That's the best sex I've ever had. I didn't know I could cum so much. For a minute there, I almost stopped you. Didn't think I could handle it, but I'm glad I didn't stop you."

"I'm glad, too!" Smooth laughed, lying down on the bed beside her.

She got down between his legs and threw his dick in her mouth. She sucked it like a pro. He started to get hard again.

"Yeah, suck that dick!"

"Mmmmm . . . Mmmmm," she moaned, only able to fit half his dick in her mouth. She tried to take more down her throat, but she started to gag, so she sucked half of it while stroking the other half with her hand. Juices flowed down her mouth and neck.

"I'm fixing to cummm," Smooth moaned out.

She picked up the speed, sucking harder. Finally, he shot his load down her throat. She didn't stop until he was bone dry.

"You taste really good," she said.

"So do you."

She slid up and cuddled next to him. Minutes later, they were both asleep.

****

Just as Smooth finished his breakfast, his cell phone rang.
"Hello?"

"Smooth, it's me, Stone. You said to call today?"

"Yeah, so how many you need?"

"I go big dis time. Give me tin."

"Alright, meet me at the usual spot at 1:00, okay?"

"I'll be der."

"Well, Rebecca, I got to go handle some business. I'll be back in a few hours."

"Okay."

"Here is a key, just in case you wanna go out."

"Yeah, I will probably take Zorro for a walk."

"Just make sure the door's locked when you leave."

"Okay."

15

Pulling up to Amanda's apartment, Smooth grabbed four kilos from the trunk, put them in a bag, closed the trunk, and then walked up to her door. After opening it, Amanda led Smooth to the kitchen as usual.

"Sorry. I just finished eating breakfast," she said.

"That's cool. So do you have those two keys done?"

"Yep. Right there in that bag," she said, pointing to a bag on one of the kitchen chairs.

"Well, here are four more I need done up."

"It will take me a few days, but I got ya."

She walked over to Smooth and kissed him. Rubbing her hands over his chest, she felt the bulletproof vest.

"See, you're still wearing it."

"Yeah. I'm not taking any chances."

She kissed him again while fumbling with his belt. He reached down and helped her with the belt and zipper. Once his pants were undone, she reached inside and pulled out his half-erect penis. She got on her knees and looked up at him while stroking his cock. Looking right into his eyes, she slid his cock in her mouth. Once he was fully erect, she started deep throating him. The way she was looking in his eyes while sucking his cock was really turning him on. So was watching his cock disappear into her mouth.

"Don't stop! I'm about to cum!" he said.

She continued sucking his cock until he came in her mouth. She swallowed every bit. After she was done, she put his cock back into his boxers, zipped up his pants, and then fixed his belt and stood up.

"How was that?" she asked.

"Awesome!"

****

Showing up at Ronny's, Smooth grabbed the bag with two keys and headed up to this door.

Knock, knock, knock . . . he tapped on the door.

Minutes later, Ronny opened it. He looked like he had just rolled out of bed.

"What time is it?" he asked.

"12:20 p.m."

"Damn, it's too early."

"Here are two more keys," Smooth said, handing the bag to Ronny.

"Here's ya money," Ronny responded, pulling a bag out from behind the couch.

"So what are your plans for the day?" Smooth asked.

"Check on all the spots. See what's popping."

"How about we go together?"

"Alright. Let me get dressed."

"I'll meet ya outside. You're driving," Smooth said, walking out the door.

He went to his trunk, opened it, and put 10 keys into one of the extra bags he kept in his trunk. Placing the bag of money in the trunk, he slammed it shut and waited for Ronny. Five minutes later, Ronny walked outside, and they then both got into Ronny's Lexus.

"First, we need to go by the gas station on 72nd Street."

"Alright."

As they pulled into the gas station, Smooth saw Stone at his usual spot leaning against his car.

"Pull up beside that car."

Smooth stepped out of the car with the bag.

"Hey Smooth."

"Waz up, Stone?"

"You see it, mon."

"Here are your ten."

"All your money's right here, mon. Tank you for dis, mon."

"No problem, Stone," Smooth responded, as they traded bags.

"I'll see ya around, Stone."

"Aw-right, mon."

Smooth got back into Ronny's car and put the money in the back seat.

"Where to now?" Ronny asked.

"It's up to you, man."

"Okay."

Ronny put on Fetty Wap's *679* and turned it up. Reaching the liquor store, Smooth saw Guru's blacked-out Charger, with Guru and Sue leaning up against it. Ronny parked next to it and they both got out. Walking around to the front of the Lexus, Smooth walked up to Sue and Guru.

"What's up?" Smooth said, giving them both dap.

"Not much," Sue responded.

"Business as usual," Guru said.

"Ya all holding it down out here?"

"Yeah. Last night two Mexicans robbed one of our spots."

"Which one?" Smooth asked.

"One on 36th Street," Guru said.

"Damn! We gotta do something about these muthafuckers!" Ronny said.

"You got that right," Sue agreed.

"Was our guy armed?" Smooth asked.

"Nah," Guru answered.

"Well, from now on, I want all of our boys strapped. Or at least one person strapped on each corner. We can't be letting these fuckers get us. Got it?"

"Yeah," Sue said.

"Yeah," Guru agreed.

"Alright, we will see ya all again soon. Come on, Ronny. Let's go check out the other spots."

Getting back into the Lexus, they headed toward their next stop. When they got to the corner store, Smooth told Ronny to pull over.

"I'm thirsty. What do you want?" Smooth asked.

"Get me a Dr. Pepper."

Smooth went into the store, got their drinks, and came back out. As they were getting ready to pull out, a low-riding Chevy Caprice pulled up with four Mexicans inside. Without a thought, Smooth pulled his FN Five-Seven pistol and hung it out the window. Smooth took aim and started firing, hitting all four of them.

He then yelled to Ronny, "Get the hell outta here!"

"Next time you decided to do that, please let me know first!"

"Sorry, wasn't thinking. But at least I got four of them. Maybe they'll learn not to fuck with us!"

"I doubt they are gonna learn. Only bad part about this war is that they have twice the numbers as we do."

"Yeah, but we're slowly picking up."

"Well, we still need more. Sue and Guru were able to help us get 15 soldiers. If we could only get 15 more..."

"By the way, Mac wants six of those tonight."

"You feeling up to partying tonight?" Smooth asked.

"Yeah, why not!"

"Say 10:00 p.m. tonight?"

"Sounds good."

"I'm gonna bring a friend with me."

"Who?"

"Rebecca. China's roommate that just got outta prison."

After checking several more spots, they went back to Ronny's.

"Remember, 10:00 p.m. tonight," Smooth reminded Ronny, before grabbing the money out of the back seat and getting out of the Lexus.

"See ya then," Ronny responded.

****

"Rebecca!" Smooth called out, as he stepped into the apartment. Zorro met him at the door with tail wagging.

"In the kitchen," Rebecca answered.

194

After bending down to pet Zorro, Smooth took a piss, washed his hands, and then went into the kitchen.

"Whacha doin'?" Smooth asked.

"Making my famous spaghetti sauce."

"Well, it smells great."

"Hope you're hungry."

"I'm starved."

"Sit down. It's almost done," Rebecca said, puling garlic bread out of the oven.

After serving Smooth his food, Rebecca made herself a plate and sat down to join him.

"This is really good," he said.

"Thanks."

"So how'd ya like to go out to a club tonight?"

"I'd love to. I haven't been to a club in five years."

"Well, there is this new place called Club Rage downtown. I do business with the owner, so he always hooks me up with V.I.P."

"What time we gonna go?"

"Be ready by 9:30 p.m. We gotta pick up my dawg, Ronny, at 10:00 p.m., and then we will go straight there."

****

At 9:15 p.m., Rebecca walked out of her room and asked, "Well, how do I look?"

She was wearing a tight Givenchy dress with a low-slung back and three-inch heels. The dress left nothing to the imagination.

"Damn, ma! You look good enough to eat!"

"I take it that you like it?"

"Hell yeah! If we weren't going somewhere, I'd be getting you out of that dress."

He'd never seen anyone look as good as her. Everyone in the club was going to be sweating her.

"You reading to go?" she asked.

"Yeah, come on!" he said, as they headed out.

Ten minutes later, they arrived at Ronny's. As soon as they pulled up, Ronny came out the door wearing a Burberry suit. As he got in the back seat, Smooth introduced them.

"Ronny, this is Rebecca. Rebecca, this is Ronny."

"Nice to meet you, Rebecca. Smooth . . . you never told me how beautiful she is."

"Don't even think about it, nigga! She's mine."

"Easy playa!" Ronny said.

As they pulled up to the club, they saw the line going all the way around the corner as usual. Smooth parked in the back beside the back door.

Ronny called Mac to let him know they were outside. While Ronny made the call, Smooth went to the trunk and pulled out the bag. After closing the trunk, he saw Ronny staring at Rebecca as she got out of the car. By the time they got to the back door, there was a bouncer holding it open for them.

"Come on in, guys. Mac's waiting," the bouncer said.

Once inside the club, Smooth asked the bouncer to escort Rebecca to V.I.P. while he and Ronny took care of business.

Entering the office, Smooth saw Mac sitting behind his desk as usual.

"How's it going, fellows?" he asked.

"Good," Smooth answered.

"Okay," Ronny said.

"Here is the 10," Smooth said, setting the bag on the desk.

"Your money is right over there," Mac said, pointing to a bag sitting on a bar in the corner.

"Alright, see ya next time," Smooth said.

"You fellows have a good time tonight," Mac said.

"Oh, we will," Ronny replied.

Smooth ran outside to put the money in his trunk while Ronny held the back door open.

"Thanks," Smooth said, as he walked back inside.

They both headed to the V.I.P. section. Rebecca had two guys up in her face. Once she saw Smooth, she broke off, went over to him, stood on her tippy toes, and kissed him.

"Let's dance," she said, as Demi Lovato's *Confident* came on.

Out on the dance floor, Rebecca was bumping and grinding all over Smooth. He was dancing with a raging hard-on. And every eye was on Rebecca. After a few songs, they headed back to V.I.P. to get drinks. It was Captain Morgan and rum for Smooth and screwdrivers for Rebecca. She seemed to be really enjoying herself.

Another woman came up and whispered something in Rebecca's ear. She broke into a big smile and said, "Be back later."

To Smooth's amazement, Rebecca and the other girl both headed out to the dance floor and started moving. Smooth sat around watching them dance. Just watching them together was getting Smooth hard. He started to imagine it being Rebecca and China.

After a few dances, Rebecca and the girl started kissing, and then they both walked over to Smooth and Rebecca introduced them.

"Smooth, this is Samantha. Samantha, this is Smooth."

"Nice to meet you, Samantha," he replied.

"Smooth, Samantha wants to come home with us tonight. Is that okay?"

Smooth looked the girl over. She looked like Jennifer Lopez . . . big ass and all.

"Yeah, that's cool."

"Let's head out now then," Rebecca suggested.

"Let me tell Ronny we leaving."

"Okay."

Looking around, Smooth spotted Ronny. He walked up to him.

"Bro, we're cutting outta here. Need a ride or ya good?"

"I'm good. Go have fun, you lucky bastard!"

Walking back to the girls, Smooth asked them if they were ready.

"Yep!" Samantha said.

"More than ready," Rebecca agreed.

Once outside, both girls climbed into the back of Smooth's car. After pulling out, Smooth looked in the rear-view mirror and saw them kissing.

****

As soon as they entered the apartment, the girls grabbed Smooth's arms and started undressing him. Once he was naked, they undressed each other. When all three were naked, they started kissing and rubbing all over each other. Rebecca started kissing Smooth, and then he felt something hot and wet wrap around his cock. Looking down, he saw Samantha sucking his dick. Before he could cum, Samantha told Rebecca to lie on the floor. Once she was on the floor, Samantha got on all fours and started eating Rebecca's pussy. Smooth got down and slid his cock in Samantha and started to fuck her while she was pleasing Rebecca. Samantha's pussy wasn't that tight, but it seemed to fit Smooth like a loose glove. He started to long-stroke her, watching his cock slide in and out of her while he heard Rebecca moan.

"Oh my God! I'm cumming!" Rebecca gasped.

Samantha stopped and lay down on the floor before Smooth could cum. It was as if they switched places. Rebecca climbed between Samantha's legs and started eating out her pussy, while putting her ass up in the air for Smooth. Smooth slid inside Rebecca's pussy. He still couldn't believe how tight she was. Smooth then started fucking her hard and fast.

"Yeah, fuck me, daddy!" Rebecca gasped, before she went back to eating Samantha's pussy.

In no time, Samantha was cumming, so Smooth picked up his pace.

"Cum deep inside of me, daddy," moaned Rebecca.

Unable to hold back any longer, he gave a groan and then exploded deep inside her.

****

The next morning, when Smooth woke up, Samantha was gone and Rebecca was in the shower. Smooth decided take Zorro for a walk. He grabbed his leash.

"Come on, boy!"

Zorro came over all excited with his tail wagging. After connecting the leash, they headed outside. On the elevator, Miranda was standing there. Once Smooth and Zorro got on, Miranda bent down to pet Zorro.

"So how's the new roommate?" she asked Smooth.

"Not as bad as I thought," he replied.

When the door opened, they headed in opposite directions.

"See ya later, Miranda."

"Yeah, same to you."

Smooth walked all the way around the block before heading back upstairs 20 minutes later. Back in the apartment, Zorro took off for the living room. Smooth followed, and when he got there, he saw Rebecca on the computer in the corner.

"Hey Smooth."

"What's up, Rebecca?"

"Did ya enjoy last night?"

"Hell yeah!"

"Wait till China gets out. It will be 10 times better!"

"I can't wait."

"Me either."

"So, what are you doing on the computer?"

"Filling out applications."

"For what?"

"To take online classes to be a nurse."

"So you decided to go legal?"

"Yeah."

"What makes you want to be a nurse?"

"Well, I love helping other people, and ever since I was a kid, I wanted to be a doctor. So a nurse is the next best thing."

"As long as that's what you want."

"It is."

16

With nothing else to do, Smooth decided to go car shopping. The Audi A4 was nice, but it was time for a new ride. So he and Ronny went out looking for something nice, but not something that screamed drug dealer. First, they stopped at a Toyota dealership. Not finding anything there, they moved on to the Kia dealership. Once again, they didn't see anything, so they moved to the Ford dealership.

"I like this Mustang, but, man, it's not really me," Smooth said.

"So, where to next?" Ronny asked.

"Might as well try out the Audi dealership."

"Yeah, but you already got an Audi," Ronny pointed out.

"Yeah, you got a point," Smooth agreed.

"How about the Dodge dealership?" Ronny suggested.

"Why not?"

After pulling into the dealership, they got out and started to look around. After 10 minutes, Smooth stepped in front of a four-door Ram 2500 that was completely blacked out.

"What do you think, Ronny?"

"It's clean and I can definitely see you in it."

"Let me test drive it," Smooth told the sales person.

"Let me go get the keys to it."

When he returned with the keys, Smooth got into the driver's seat, the sales associate sat in the passenger seat, and Ronny jumped in the backseat.

"Nice and comfortable," Ronny said.

"Yeah, lots of leg room," the sales person offered.

Easing out of the parking lot, Smooth decided to see what the sucker could do. He stomped down on the gas. He burned rubber coming out of the lot sideways, leaving a trail of rubber.

"Now that's what I'm talking about," Smooth exclaimed.

After driving around the block, Smooth decided to buy it. While completing the paperwork back at the dealership, the sales person asked if he was looking to buy or lease the truck.

"Buy," Smooth replied.

"How much are you looking to pay a month?" the sales person asked.

"I'll pay $500 a month. I got $10,000 right now as a down payment."

Smooth had enough cash to buy 100 trucks, but this was a way to build up his credit score for the future.

"Which insurance company?" the sales person asked.

"Farmers."

After all the paperwork was completed, Smooth and Ronny were standing beside his new truck.

"Thanks for helping me out," Smooth said.

"No problem. Anytime," Ronny replied.

Catch up with ya later then," Smooth said, giving Ronny dap.

As Smooth was pulling out of the car dealership, his phone rang.

"Hello?"

"This is a collect call from China, an inmate at Lowell Correctional Institution. To accept the call, press zero."

Smooth pressed zero.

"This call may be monitored and/or recorded. Thanks for using Securus."

"Hey baby!" Smooth said.

"Hey. What ya doing?"

"Just bought a new truck."

"What's up with the Audi?"

"Figured I'd let Rebecca use it."

"Bet she'd like that."

"I'm gonna be up to see ya next weekend."

"Not this week?"

"Nah, because GaGa and Roxy will be there. Figured I'd let ya all have a girl day."

"Okay. That sounds good."

"How are ya on money?"

"I'm straight."

"I ordered you a package on line. Did you get it?"

"Yeah, I got it. Thanks baby."

"You're welcome."

"I love you," she said.

"I love you more. And I miss you like crazy."

"You have one minute left," the automated voice announced.

"Tell Rebecca that I love and miss her, and I will call her tonight."

"Alright. Love ya," he told her, before hanging up.

****

Opening the door, Zorro barked and came running. His tail was going nuts.

"Hey boy!" Smooth said, bending down to pet him. When he got to the living room, he saw Rebecca on the computer.

"Hey Rebecca, what are you doing?" he asked.

"School work. Why, what's up?"

"Talked to China. She says she loves you and will call you tonight."

"Okay."

"Also, I went car shopping today and bought a new truck. So here . . ." he said, throwing his Audi keys to her. "Now you got your own wheels. I already put you on my insurance, so now you got your own car and don't have to depend on me to drive you around."

"Thank you so much. And that private detective, Mr. Nick Ferro, called and had good news. He found my brother for me. He gave me his phone number so I actually got to call and talk to him."

"So, how's he doing?"

"He's great. And the best part is that he's living here in Miami. I'm gonna meet up with him tonight. I want him to come over and meet you. Is that okay?"

"Yeah, that's fine. Invite him over."

****

Later that night, Smooth and Rebecca were on the couch watching T.V. when there was a knock at the door.

Rebecca jumped up and yelled, "I got it!"

A minute later, she walked into the living room and announced, "Smooth, this is my brother, E . . . ."

Before she could say his name, the guy stuck out his hand to shake hands and said, "Just call me Spencer. Everyone else does."

"Well, it's nice to meet you, Spencer," Smooth said, shaking his hand.

"Same here," Spencer replied.

"Your sister tells me you were in the military."

"Yeah, I just got out."

"What'd you do?"

"I was infantry."

"Why'd you get out?"

"'Cause I realized there's a lot more money in the private sector."

"I can see that. So now you're what, a hired gun . . . as they say?"

"I guess you could call it that."

"Would you like something to drink?"

"Sure, what do you have?"

"Rum, vodka, juice, or Coke."

"How about rum with a little Coke."

"Alright, I'll make the drinks while you two catch up."

Smooth headed to the kitchen taking his time so they would have a little more time to catch up.

After several drinks and lots of talking, Smooth said, "Well, I'm gonna hit the sack and let you all have some privacy. Spencer, it was nice meeting you. Please feel free to sleep on the couch."

"Thanks."

"Goodnight, babe," Rebecca said.

****

China was sitting at the poker table playing a card game called Skin when she noticed a girl cheating.

"Bitch is cheating!" China exclaimed.

"Who you calling a bitch?"

"You!" China said, as she slapped the girl.

"Oh, it's on now, bitch!"

"Get to the room then," China ordered.

China headed to the room, with the girl following her.

"I'm gonna teach you a lesson," the girl said, as she took a swing at China.

China sidestepped and punched the girl right in the nose. Blood shot out everywhere. The girl tried to tackle China and they both fell to the floor. China then flipped the girl off of her, climbed on top of her, and started punching the girl. Left, right, left, right. China continued to beat the shit out her, until she felt someone punch her in the back three times. The pain was blinding. China reached behind her and felt warm wetness. Pulling her hand back and looking at it, it was covered in blood. The room started to spin.

China's last thought was that someone had stabbed her. Then her world got blank . . . dark . . . finished.

****

Smooth woke up the next morning and found Rebecca pacing the living room floor.

207

"What's wrong?" Smooth asked.
"You might want to sit down."
"Why?"

TO BE CONTINUED . . .

BOOKS BY GOOD2GO AUTHORS

GOOD 2 GO FILMS PRESENTS

**THE HAND I WAS DEALT- FREE WEB SERIES
NOW AVAILABLE ON YOUTUBE!
YOUTUBE.COM/SILKWHITE212**

SEASON TWO NOW AVAILABLE

To order books, please fill out the order form below:

To order films please go to *www.good2gofilms.com*

Name:_____

Address:_____

City: _____ State: _____ Zip Code: _____

Phone:_____

Email:_____

Method of Payment: Check   VISA   MASTERCARD

Credit Card#:_____

Name as it appears on card: _____

Signature: _____

Item Name	Price	Qty	Amount
48 Hours to Die – Silk White	$14.99		
Business Is Business – Silk White	$14.99		
Business Is Business 2 – Silk White	$14.99		
Business Is Business 3 – Silk White	$14.99		
Childhood Sweethearts – Jacob Spears	$14.99		
Childhood Sweethearts 2 – Jacob Spears	$14.99		
Flipping Numbers – Ernest Morris	$14.99		
Flipping Numbers 2 – Ernest Morris	$14.99		
He Loves Me, He Loves You Not - Mychea	$14.99		
He Loves Me, He Loves You Not 2 - Mychea	$14.99		
He Loves Me, He Loves You Not 3 - Mychea	$14.99		
He Loves Me, He Loves You Not 4 – Mychea	$14.99		
He Loves Me, He Loves You Not 5 – Mychea	$14.99		
Lost and Turned Out – Ernest Morris	$14.99		
Married To Da Streets – Silk White	$14.99		
My Besties – Asia Hill	$14.99		
My Besties 2 – Asia Hill	$14.99		
My Besties 3 – Asia Hill	$14.99		
My Besties 4 – Asia Hill	$14.99		
My Boyfriend's Wife - Mychea	$14.99		
My Boyfriend's Wife 2 – Mychea	$14.99		
Never Be The Same – Silk White	$14.99		
Stranded – Silk White	$14.99		
Slumped – Jason Brent	$14.99		
Tears of a Hustler - Silk White	$14.99		
Tears of a Hustler 2 - Silk White	$14.99		
Tears of a Hustler 3 - Silk White	$14.99		
Tears of a Hustler 4- Silk White	$14.99		
Tears of a Hustler 5 – Silk White	$14.99		
Tears of a Hustler 6 – Silk White	$14.99		
The Panty Ripper - Reality Way	$14.99		
The Panty Ripper 3 – Reality Way	$14.99		

The Teflon Queen – Silk White	$14.99		
The Teflon Queen 2 – Silk White	$14.99		
The Teflon Queen 3 – Silk White	$14.99		
The Teflon Queen 4 – Silk White	$14.99		
The Teflon Queen 5 – Silk White	$14.99		
Time Is Money - Silk White	$14.99		
Young Goonz – Reality Way	$14.99		
Subtotal:			
Tax:			
Shipping (Free) U.S. Media Mail:			
Total:			

Make Checks Payable To:
Good2Go Publishing
7311 W Glass Lane,
Laveen, AZ 85339

CPSIA information can be obtained
at www.ICGtesting.com
Printed in the USA
LVHW031544220919
631868LV00010B/501/P

9 781943 686605